BELAJANE CRILLY

The Ship, The Keep, and the Kingdom

ORPHANS AND DRAGON

St. Charles IL

Library of Congress Control Number:2024900970

First edition

ISBN: 979-8-9898969-2-9

This book was professionally typeset on Reedsy.
Find out more at reedsy.com

for Charlie and CeCe,
Land Girls extraordinaire.

Though oft a tale may seem complete,
And have an ending oh so neat,
A tale of war is never done;
With each new player, the web is spun.
Like dervishes, between the pages
Spin yet more sparring, spitting, ages.
Those once friends may now be foes,
Yet this is the least of battle's woes.
Echoes of the past fade swift,
Fore-showing things to come, their parting gift.

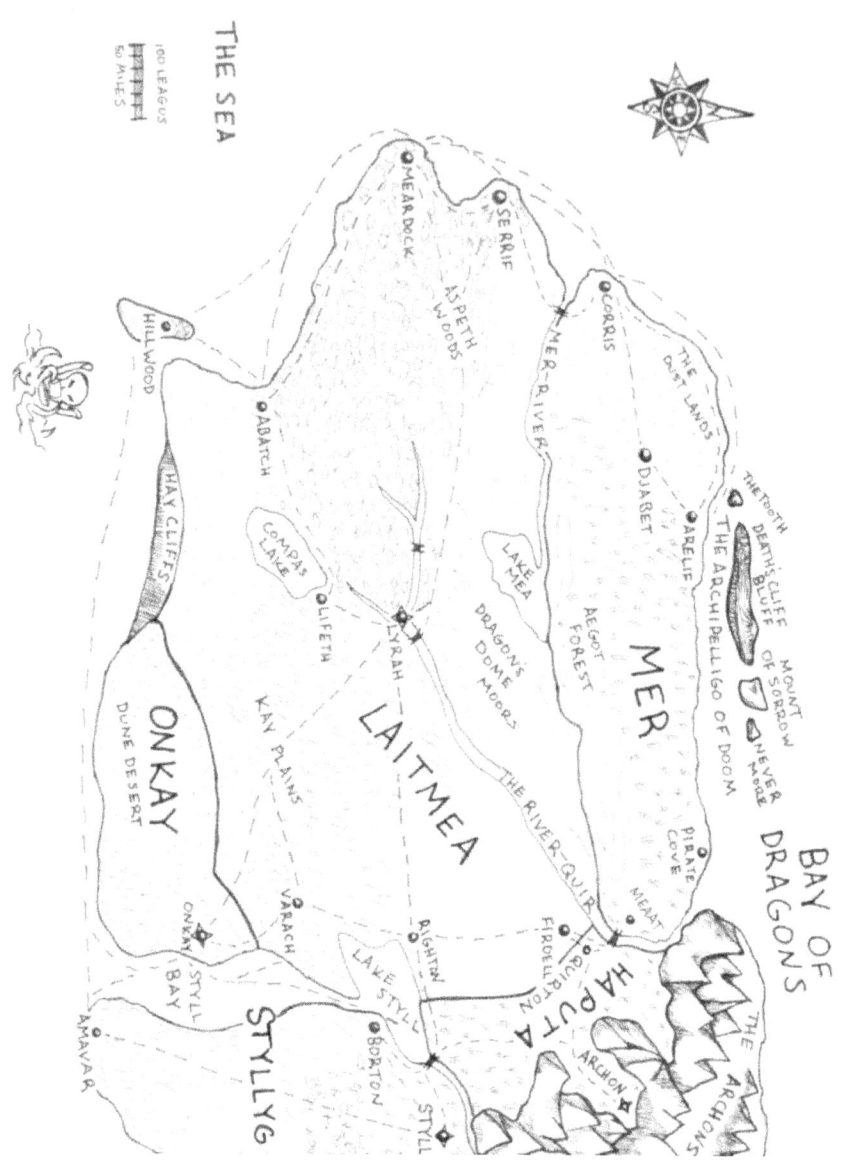

Prologue

Katjia

The war had been done five years when Katjia was born, but everyone still talked about it. Her older brother, Kanara, said she was lucky to only hear. He had been but three then, and what he remembered still made him scream at night. He was not the only one, either.

She watched his hunched shoulders now, as he rode ahead of her in procession, taut with anger and fear even when awake. He would have been a pretty boy, with hair thicker and longer than hers, a good strong chin, and even, white teeth. But Katjia didn't have to see to know that the cleft between his eyebrows was growing deeper with every passing mile.

As the sad monotony of her horse's plodding allowed her mind to drift, she found herself in the midst of a memory she had no wish to recall.

She had been small, too small to really understand, when she had asked her father why Kanara cried out in the night. It was the only question she had ever asked him, and his hard, angry voice still rang in her ears.

"Laitmea sucked us like a leech. Sixteen years, until all the blood ran out of us, and Onkay was as dry as the desert at noon. So, we did not resist. They said it would be easier that way. Easier, with no food and less hope and soldiers taking whatever they pleased? And if you did resist, keep a round of bread to feed your children, what did you get? A slap to the face, if you were lucky, your head rolling in the sand, if you were not. Ah, well, fewer mouths to feed.

"So, we were not like Haputa, with plague running rampant and battles in the

street. So, we died lying down, while they died standing up. And when vengeance was finally had, won by others, handed to us over the mangled corpse of our dignity, what do we get? Our slaves back, tens, out of the thousands that they killed, and money.

"Can money rebuild the scattered herd? Horses were our life, herds a thousand strong, ours bred of lines as old as the desert itself. They had a longer and more noble lineage than the royal family of our conquerors. Money does not buy those horses. They are passed from mother to daughter and father to son. They live as we live and die as we die, and any one at market would fetch ten times the price of Laitmeas' horses, and a thousand times what they paid us, because that horse was born and bred in the lands of our people! It will be lifetimes before our herds are built back to their zenith, if we can survive at all. Our way of life has been shattered beyond all repair."

A child cried out behind her, lifting Katjia from her reverie. One of her small cousins, she discerned, from the babble of shushing and hushing that followed. She did not turn around to see. Neither did Kanara. She understood his pain far better now.

She was fifteen, a young woman, able to cope with adult sorrows and secrets, but as often as not, her brother did not want her understanding. He was a world away in his own thoughts now, and it was best to leave him be. She still worried about him though, whether he liked it or not. Twenty-three was quite old for an unmarried man, even in a desert life where things moved slowly. Twenty three was, on the other hand, quite young to be the head of a household with an ailing mother, an unwed sister, three dependent widowed aunts, and nineteen young cousins ranging in age from two to fourteen.

Kanara had wept and fretted about his new responsibility when their father had died, but with the passing of each of his uncles in turn, the cleft between his eyebrows just got deeper. And now famine. Was it any surprise, really, that their people were starving? The desert had little to offer, even to those who knew its every secret.

Onkay had exactly one city of note, a glorified encampment on the edge of the grasslands, the only place with water enough to support year-round habitation. City dwellers had, at one time, been treated as lepers by her kind.

No honest people would tie themselves to the same tract of land, year in and year out.

Katjia's nomadic brethren wandered the dunes from season to season, spiraling through different oases in a dance older than time. So it had been. But then the rains had not come, and the grass on the edge of Setting-Sun Pool had not come up. They had turned around and trekked back to another spring, but it was the same everywhere. No rain, no grass. The mare's milk had dried up, the foals were few and thin, and everyone was hungry. The Horse Lords of Onkay fled to the city.

First only a few, families they had called weak, who did not know how to endure. Then a year had passed, and another, and the few who remained began to look east, towards the place called civilization. And even in the city, it was said, there was not enough. Too many, too many had come. Her family was the oldest, and the strongest, and the last to leave.

No, thought Katjia, *We are the last to go because we are stubborn. Being old and strong was no reason to stay. Pride is what kept us here, beyond hope.* Only when father's youngest brother had died, and all his responsibility fallen on Kanara, was a decision reached.

The last Horse Lords would leave their desert home, but not for the city of Onkay. It was far too late to find a place in those overgrazed pastures.

Kanara had made up his mind suddenly, or so it had seemed to the others. Katjia knew how long he had thought on it, since before her Uncle's death. Even if he had never told her, she would have known what he was thinking. The day of their Uncle's burying, he had taken her aside and asked her thoughts on leaving.

"I think," he had said, "that it is what our father would do, but I am terribly afraid anyway."

"You don't have to be just like father. As long as you do your very best to lead us, you will not be a failure," she had snapped, perhaps less caring than she should have been.

Oh, they had talked about leaving. But she saw the pain in his eyes and knew that the thing weighing heavy on his heart was what they never talked about and never would. Gynn. The child their parents had borne after Kanara and before Katjia. A little girl who had died before she was old enough for a proper name. The reason Kanara screamed in his sleep. His fear that one day she too would die like Gynn.

"If it comforts you to think that this is what father would do as well, then by all means, be it so." It was little enough consolation, but it had worked. A season later, they were leaving. Leaving the desert behind, and going to Laitmea, a country long their enemy, now their only hope.

* * *

KATJIA

Veena

I have been told to keep an account of the things I have learned and the adventures I shall have. It was my Uncle's idea, and the purpose is twofold. One, so that I shall not forget all the lessons, remedies, and words of advice that others have taught me. Two, so that we have a permanent record of my achievements, so that no details may be overlooked. I shall endeavor to keep it faithfully.

* * *

My Uncle has told me to write down the names and histories of the important members of our party. He thinks this is vital information. I do not. There are two thousand of us, quite possibly more, and so to write about all of them would take years. I complained, and so he told me to explain the orders of pirates and then only give the histories of their leaders. I still think this is a ridiculous exercise, and I have far better ways to spend my time, but Uncle was adamant, so I shall begin.

Our King is Zavaxer. He rules over all the pirates. In other words, his duties include settling any disputes that we cannot settle among ourselves, deciding whether or not new members may be accepted, and telling us when, where, and from whom we may take our spoils. Anyone can challenge him at any time for the title, but if they lose the ensuing duel, they die. Zavaxer has been king for fourteen years now, the longest anyone has remained king, after he challenged and killed the former king, Leopold. Zavaxer himself has been challenged five times and, obviously, he has won each time.

Although we pirates are mostly unified, we do have a few different groups or orders, as they have come to be known. As we are not a very original bunch, they are merely called the First, Second, and Third orders.

The First Order is made up mostly of those who are staunch loyalists to our present king. None of these members challenge him, and they always defend the king if an argument breaks out against him.

The King typically calls upon the wisest members of this order to give him advice, so I suppose they form a sort of council, though they are never called such. Anyone may join or leave at any time, so the members of this "council" change frequently. Members of the First Order not chosen to be "council" members are raiders. Most are men between the ages of fifteen and forty. The leader of this order is, of course, the King.

The Second Order is made up of those pirates who are either too old, too weak, or too young to join the raiding parties. These people are usually assigned menial tasks, such as taking care of livestock, cooking, doing laundry, and repairing our homes or ships. A few of these are doctors, such as my Uncle, and there are also some who are old enough and have earned enough respect to be comfortably taken care of by the other members of this order for the remainder of their lives. In fact, my Uncle currently leads this order, although he still answers to the king. I am a member of this order as well, since my Uncle would not give his consent for me to join the raiding parties.

Carsten is the leader of a minority of pirates who call themselves the Third Order, though they are not formally recognized by the First Order. They are mostly raiders and such who are officially part of the First Order, but this growing group is primarily made up of men between the ages of fifteen and twenty-two. Members of this order are watched carefully by the council, for while they claim loyalty to King Zavaxer, they have been known to go against his instructions. They have never been officially found guilty of wrongdoing, disobedience, or treason against the King, but they are still an unruly lot.

2

And now that I have finished this long and completely unnecessary task, I shall retire.

* * *

Uncle was pleased with what I have written so far, but was rather cross that I left my own history out of it. I reminded him that he told me only to write of the leaders and their Orders, but he said that as the author, I should explain who I am and how I came to be here.

I don't really see what this has to do with anything, and I told him so in no uncertain terms. Uncle merely smiled, remaining infuriatingly calm as always, and told me to start writing.

My name is Veena. I have no other. My father and his brother were captured during a pirate raid on Haputa when they were young, and were made to join. My Uncle grew to enjoy the lifestyle and became the best medic in all of Eretz. However my father, Steph, despised it and eventually ran away with my mother, a Laitmean peasant by the name of Serafina.

We don't take kindly to traitors, though, so they were pursued and recaptured some months later. My father was killed immediately, but the pirates spared my mother as it was apparent that she was by that time with child. I was born on the fifth day of Winter and my mother died a few hours later that same day.

Uncle raised me. He trained me to be useful to the pirates. Consequently, I cook, clean, do laundry, occasionally keep records, aid my Uncle with his medical practices, and spy.

I hesitated to write any more, but Uncle says it's all right. He has a good hiding place for this record and if it is ever in danger of being found he will destroy it. I told him that it had better not be found because if he destroys all of my hard work, I will be extraordinarily upset.

At any rate, I am a very valuable spy as I look enough like my parents to pass as either a Laitmean or a Haputian, and I can imitate the accent of either nation. I don't even have a branding to hide since I'm not part of the raiding party. I have yet to be sent out on a formal mission, but Uncle keeps hinting that the time may be coming soon, thus his insistence that I begin this record. He claims things will stick in my head better if I write them down, and while I suppose he is right, I would sooner leave the pirates than give him the satisfaction of knowing I thought so.

* * *

Veena

Uncle read that last part even though I told him not to. If he is making me keep this foolish record, the least he can do is respect my privacy when I actually write my own thoughts. He also told me that I forgot to mention my age. I still don't see what that has to do with anything, but fine. I AM SEVENTEEN!

* * *

A List of Common Ailments and their Cures
By: Veena

Headache: a tea of willow and mint, and lavender rubbed to the temples will cure nearly every headache.

Fever: fever-few, willow, lemon balm, or ginger (consumed) will help to take down a fever, as will applying cold compresses when available.

Chills: cinnamon, garlic, or ginger (consumed).

Toothache: cloves, yarrow, or cayenne (consumed.)

Cramps: mint or lavender, when applied to the cramp, will help to soothe it, as will consuming lemon balm or chamomile tea.

Swelling: thyme and ginger made into a tea and consumed will help, as will ice or a cold compress applied to the area.

Cuts, wounds, and heavy bleeding: apply pressure and bind wound with clean fabric, (boiled preferable). Thyme or chamomile consumed as tea will also help. For large wounds, pack tightly with cattail fluff. Change binding every other day.

Plague (not as common as it once was, but since so many who have it come to Uncle, we see it frequently): ginger, cinnamon, yarrow, dandelion, and lemon balm tea (consumed) will help with some symptoms, as will, of course, resting and applying cold compresses.

Little can be done to prevent nerve damage once the disease has already progressed. It is best to avoid drinking from foreign bodies of water. If this is not possible, boil the water before consumption, as this seems to reduce sickness.

* * *

Questions to Ask and Things to Say to Get People to Reveal More Than
They Intend
By: Veena

- Interesting!
- Really?
- Is that so?
- Do tell!
- How peculiar!
- How exciting!
- You must have been/felt ____

- What do you mean?
- What do you think?
- Do you believe ____?
- What would the King/Queen say?
- Do you agree?
- Is it a secret?
- Why?/Why not?

* * *

Essentials for Journeys or Missions
By: Veena

Food:

- Dried fruits and meat
- Water
- Avoid cooking supplies and foods that need to be cooked when possible

Clothing:

- Only bring extra if absolutely necessary
- Be sure clothing has places to conceal weapons.

Money:

- Small amounts
- Hide in secret pockets.
- Carry a small but believable amount to pacify robbers without making them suspicious

Medicine:

- Bandages
- Lavender
- Extra water (besides drinking water, you may have to wash wounds, apply compresses.)

These are the absolute essentials. Most anything else can be found on the road

* * *

Other Tips

- Pack as lightly as possible
- Always carry a concealed weapon
- Always have a stated reason for the journey (if the real one ought not to be common knowledge)
- Dress and act as the natives of the area to avoid suspicion
- Never hurt or kill another person unless they are a danger to you or your mission

* * *

Mayzin

My dearest twin brother has challenged me to keep a diary for one year, as we are now fourteen years old, and that was the age our mother first kept a diary at. I tried to tell him that such things are childish and silly, and that keeping a diary in no way guarantees we will have grand adventures like mother did, but he seemed so excited about the prospect that I suppose I shall humor him.

I shall not, however, repurpose my sketchbook, as he has. Our governess would be most displeased, and school books are not fit for diaries anyway. I have purchased a proper journal, as well as a spare quill and some extra ink. So now I shall set about this writing business properly.

My name is Lady Mayzin Avilamin Della of Lyrah, and I am the third youngest child of Princess Quipeneay of Lyrah and Prince Captain of the Guard Redgenold of Lyrah. My elder siblings are Lara, age nineteen, Redge, age eighteen, Kestly, age seventeen, Xeno, age sixteen, and Quipeneay, (Pippy,) age fifteen.

Myself and my twin, Marley, are fourteen, although I am a hair older. The baby of the family is Jessimin, our thirteen-year-old sister. The lot of us are as blond as can be, save Pippy, who has tomato red hair. I think she gets that from father's side of the family. Reggie's and Jessi's and my eyes are blue, everyone else in the family has green.

Lots of people think that Marley is touched in the head because he only ever talks about ships and sailing, but he only looks crazy. We've been together since before we were born, so I should know. Kestly can be as mad as mother sometimes but, never my Marley.

Now that I have given an account of my age and looks, I suppose the other important things must go down. My parents are good friends with the King and Queen of Laitmea, my mother being the Queen's personal guard. Lara and Reggie and Pippy would leave it at that, but it's not the whole truth.

My parents and the Queen were born in Haputa, and came to power after they helped end the seventeen-year conflict between Haputa and Laitmea. My Queen, Trilliapa, in addition to being a brilliant leader and dragon rider, is also a common thief. My King Dowlin and my mother conspired to kill the former king, Darin. My father joined the army he now runs under false pretenses, and my mother and the Queen are sworn subjects of the Pirates of Mer.

What have I forgotten? Oh yes. My mother is a little insane. And that is the whole, messy truth. Actually, by the standards of Laitmean aristocracy, my family is boring. Lady Arabell of Lifeth has my mother beat by ten on the madness count, and her youngest daughter Bellanne (Bella) has been hinting that she's going to run away with the stable-hand.

Arabell's daughter actually asked if I would cover for her - ask her to stay with me so that she can go and marry him in secret without anyone getting suspicious. I said that I would—I post the letter to her tomorrow. I keep all of her letters in here, so Jessi must never find this journal, or there will be so much gossip I'll never be able to show my face in court again.

I know that a few years back, Lady Etaklare of Meardock left her diary where her maid found it, and there was such a scandal when its contents got out that she gave up her title and moved to Onkay. I don't know what Marley expected me to put in a diary, but I'm sure it wasn't this!

* * *

To my friend, (if I can call you that) Mayzin,
From Bella of Lifeth.
My mother has stopped bleating like a goat—thanks for asking. I had a grand

time with you at that midsummer ball, even if everyone kept shooting me sidelong glances—like I would start bleating too. I'm just writing to say that it has happened! Finny finally asked me to marry him!! If you could send that letter we talked about? I am over the moon with joy right now—I know why you questioned my decision to fall in love with "the horse poop boy," but I don't care right now! Send the letter!

If you want to admonish me, wait six months. The glamour will have worn off by then, and I'll probably be sick of living in a one-room hut, and longing for my jewels and combs. But oh, just think! I'll be free of all the funny looks and questions about mother! And I get Finny, with those muscles of his! You should try falling in love with a horse poop boy sometime! It would do you good.

Sincerely, Bella

* * *

To Bella of Lifeth,

From Mayzin

Well, I'm going to post the letter. You have one week to repent. If I don't hear otherwise, I shall assume that you are still running away with Finny and wish you luck!

I'm glad to hear that your mother is doing better. Mine's the same as always. As for falling in love with a horse poop boy, I'll consider it, but there aren't any good specimens at the palace right now. But you never know. It'll be two years before I can be foisted upon some nobleman, and perhaps father will hire someone good looking in time.

I do think that I would be stealing your claim to fame though, if I picked a stable-hand. Perhaps my Finny shall turn out to be a butler, or a coachman. I'll be hard-pressed to beat my big brother though! Let's not forget that Xeno has been talking of marrying the baker's daughter!

Sincerely, Mayzin

* * *

To her ladyship, Arabell of Lifeth,

I am writing to request your daughter's presence at a small luncheon I am holding. If her ladyship is amenable, Bella should come to my residence next Saturday, and return Monday morning.

Many thanks,

Lady Mayzin of Lyrah

* * *

Veena

King Zavaxer has selected my Uncle and me for a mission of utmost importance. We are to be a delegation to the King, and more importantly, Queen of Laitmea. It will be our job to convey his greetings and his displeasure with their conduct.

By our law, the Queen and her Lady are still pirates of the First Order, yet they have pretended that they no longer bear any affiliation to us. Thus far, messages to the contrary have fallen on deaf ears, and the King now believes that things have gone too far.

Laitmea has begun to wage a war of sorts on us, preventing us not only from seizing their ships, but the ships of other countries as well. Zavaxer believes that it is time to remind them of where their loyalties lie.

Of course, we pirates are not a properly recognized foreign entity. Any Laitmean school child could tell you as much. The seat of government in Mer is inland, in the city of Djabet. Ostensibly.

In truth, whoever rules the Pirates' Cove rules Mer. There is a puppet government in the capital, but they control nothing more than a dusty crossroads between impassible forests and the Dust Lands. Occasionally, they send envoys to other nations, or rather, they ask Zavaxer to send one of the Second Order to pacify our neighbors. The real politicians all know this, and of late, Laitmea has even been sending letters directly here by ship, rather than over land through Djabet.

The reason for this is simple: we in Mer do not have the resources nor the desire to form great cities inland, where the air is so dry that one can die of dehydration in a few hours. In the west, there is enough sea breeze to keep a few outposts furnished, but unlike the desert nomads of Onkay, those in the Dust Lands do not have the luxury of ground springs or oases to travel between. It is not a true desert, full of sand, for the damp fog off the sea supports a tough kind of grass. The dryness is mainly a result of the bitter cold. I have never witnessed it, but Uncle has said that at night in the Dust Lands, it becomes so cold that a cup of hot tea spilled from shoulder height will turn to ice before the droplets touch the ground.

South of the Dust Lands, there is no one to spill a cup of tea. The forest that grows there is too dense, dark, and full of dragons to even think of crossing. Only in the archipelago is there a greater density of the winged monsters, for the ocean currents stop it from becoming so bitterly cold there. (Incidentally, this is why Laitmea never truly moved against us during the seventeen-year's war.)

Thus, our civilization is concentrated along the coasts, and our only trade of note is by sea. While the bulk of the population here are not pirates, most citizens have a great respect for us. We do not attack our own, and for small gifts of food or fuel, we will even offer the layman protection from any bandit of the sea or land.

* * *

My Uncle says that now we are on the road, and there is no chance at all of someone reading this account, I should write of our true purpose on this mission. He will keep this book on his person, and should anyone threaten us, he shall destroy it immediately.

Had anyone found my account up to this point, it would have been extremely difficult, but not impossible, to explain away. Now we enter the realm of high treason. I have protested mightily against recording anything regarding this journey, but as always, Uncle's reasoning is sound.

Due to the nature of our mission, it is absolutely imperative that I remember every detail of every encounter we have. It is yet more critical that I remember the lies I must tell, so that I am not caught contradicting myself. It has already proven true that the act of writing crystallizes things in my mind like nothing else, and when, eventually, we are lauded as heroes among our own, our endeavors will be a celebrated addition to pirate lore.

I believe that last bit to be unnecessary hyperbole on my Uncle's part, but I will continue my account nonetheless.

Neither my Uncle nor I truly serve King Zavaxer. While we are leading the Second Order, our true allegiance is to the Third Order. In a way, I have been a spy for the better part of three years already, performing duties for the Second Order, while informing the Third Order of important details of Laitmea's communications which King Zavaxer wouldn't trust them with.

I came to this job as a matter of course, because I am unobtrusive, courteous, and loyal, so council members often share information around me that even Uncle would not hear. I am also the only person Uncle trusts completely, for I am his own flesh and blood. His secrets are safe with me.

My Uncle began hand picking men to lead the Third Order at the beginning of King Zavaxer's reign, though outwardly he seems to be one of the King's strongest supporters. He was in a unique position to do so, because any member of any order is free to seek a private conversation with him, and it will all be put down as a medical concern. The reason for all of this cloak-and-dagger secrecy and treason is simplicity itself.

King Zavaxer wants peace with Laitmea. He first challenged Leopold for precisely that reason. His arguments are that we are too few to go against the wishes of so mighty a nation, regardless of the Queen and her Lady breaking every oath they swore to us. He says we must content ourselves with leeching off whatever meager fare sails by that does not have affiliation with the crown. He would leave us with little more than scraps, jeopardizing our way of life for the sake of cowardliness and loyalty to a Queen who was a low level raider for one season, twenty years ago. He ought to have known that these policies would turn my Uncle against him, but he is nothing if not a fool. He has continued to kowtow to more and more audacious requests of the Laitmean government.

15

My Uncle is, of course, infuriated, but not so much as me, I think. He had the pleasure of knowing the Queen and her Lady whilst they were still here. Apparently, they are *almost* worthy of Zavaxer's fear. He was also able to see Laitmea's capital under their rule, as he and my father were Mer's delegation to the peace talks at the end of the seventeen-year's war. It was after the treaty signing that my father left the order and escaped into the Laitmean countryside.

Uncle has argued for years that his little brother's traitorous betrayal should nullify Mer's involvement in the peace contracts, but since he was still a pirate at the time he signed, there was little to be done about that. So we now work with the Third Order in hopes of escaping from the long arm of Laitmean power. King Zavaxer would trust few with this mission to bring peace between nations. Luckily, my Uncle and I are the best. Uncle has the added benefit of knowing the royals personally, from his doctoring days. Hopefully, this means that they trust him almost as much as Zavaxer does. But back to high treason.

King Zavaxer is correct in his assertions that we are too few to directly engage Laitmea. However, there are ways of altering their government's stance towards us that do not involve all-out war. A few targeted attacks, some sleight of hand, and a well-placed spy will grant us all the freedoms we might wish for, treaty or no.

While my Uncle bargains for 'peace,' I will be left to explore Laitmea's capital. This will give me ample opportunity to casually run into several key players in our plot. I currently have one contact among the Laitmean aristocracy. This person's identity must not be revealed, even here, for reasons which will ultimately become clear. Suffice it to say, this individual reached out to the Second Order several years ago and was able to provide sufficient proof of their identity and motives to ensure our trust. I have since become a go-between, among my other duties, and we have struck up a healthy correspondence.

My contact has provided the name of a worthy candidate for the Laitmean throne, one who would respect our wishes, should the current King and Queen be deposed. My contact's candidate is also high-ranking in Laitmea, but must remain ignorant of our plot. If the candidate knows that he is in position to claim the crown, he could give us away. He will be informed of our intentions when it it time for him to take the throne. We will need to overthrow the government without his assistance. To this end, my contact has also provided the necessary information to go about this coup.

By far the easiest way to take out the royal family would be to have their own people oust them. With only about a thousand fighting men, the Third Order is in poor position for military takeover. So we come to the convoluted, but elegant solution. The Queen and her Lady, unfit to rule as they are, are not the only ones with shady pasts. If the full truth of Darin the Terrible's rise and demise were to be made public, chances are, all the landed gentry would be leaving in disgrace. The only issue is that all the records of the King and Queen's own treason are locked up in the palace keep, guarded by a dragon.

In order for someone to steal all of the requisite letters and whatnot, quite a large distraction would be needed. Just the sort of distraction, in fact, that one thousand hostile men would make. But simply attacking is not the answer. Somebody needs to be on the inside when this distraction happens, and if possible it would be best for the royal family not to suspect foul play on the part of the pirates. And here, my informant had the answer: Redgenold, son of Lord Captain of the Guard Redgenold, second child of the mad Quip. Possibly the only person in existence as deranged as his mother.

* * *

Marley

When my mother was fourteen years old she kept a diary, which, as luck would have it, now contains one of only a few accurate accounts of the events leading up to the death of King Darin the Terrible.

The whole story is not widely known, and from start to finish it was an odd business. When I learned of it, I thought it would be grand fun for me to keep a diary. As my sister Mayzin points out, I am not likely to become involved in piracy, war, spying, or assassinations, but one can hope.

As the seventh of eight highborn children, I have little to look forward to in life. My oldest brother, of course, gets dibs on any foreign princesses that need to get married, and pirate attacks are few and far between this far in land.

Mayzin at least enjoys being in court, gossiping and flirting and the like. I, however, am in a state of perpetual mortification, and I dread the coming of my sixteenth birthday like other children dread the pox.

I'm fourteen now, and not growing younger, so it is unavoidable, but I hope that I can arrange to move out of the country before then. Mayzin is my twin sister, and very pretty, with long golden curls and father's blue eyes.

It's hard to understand why I would dread coming of age, when I'm almost as handsome as her, but then, almost is not quite *as*. While she'll get snapped up by some noble or other the minute she's old enough to wed, I'll be lucky if any girl will stand within ten feet of me, let alone agree to marry me.

I have all the social graces of a turtle. I know that I have a reputation for being a little strange, but I can't help it when everyone has created such bizarre rules for social conduct. I don't much like talking, dancing, or any of the horribly noisy parties that everyone is so found of throwing. But everything from work to weddings to weekends in the countryside seems to hinge upon endless conversation. I just don't have that much to say, and unfortunately, I'm not quite muscular enough to be considered strong and silent. I'm just quiet and odd.

To make matters worse, I don't even have some suitably stodgy noble father and dumpy mother. While Lord Captain of the Guard and Queen's Lady might sound regal, Ma and Pa are anything but.

At the last midsummer feast, when Mayzin was dozing off at the table, and most everyone had cleared out, they began to duel with their butter knives. Not silly little taps either. They mounted the table, stood astride the empty gravy boat and a tureen still full of peas, and jousted like knights in full battle.

I'm not some snotty noble with too much gold who thinks of nothing but etiquette, but any fool can see that I'm in a pickle. I only hope that my fortune changes for the better—or at least more exciting and less embarrassing.

* * *

Veena

Uncle says that I must learn to write more quickly. I say that if he wanted a short explanation, he should have devised a more simple plan.

I am to find and seduce the young Redgenold; not a hard task, I would assume, given his age and my rather stunning beauty, but still, I must tread carefully. I shall convince him that, even though he is twelfth in line for the throne, he really ought to be king. I don't want to marry a simple *prince* after all. I will then arrange for him to attempt his own coup with the men of the Third Order. With everyone suitably distracted, and the horrendous dragon away defending his mistress, it will be a simple matter of stealing the requisite paperwork, and making a run for it.

Redgenold's little insurrection will of course be crushed, and my informant's *suitable candidate* will receive the praise for dispatching the dangerous threat to the peace. Then everything the royal family has tried to keep hidden away will be thrown into the light, and we pirates will see the dawn of a golden age.

Sympathetic Laitmean leadership will allow us rich plunder beyond our wildest dreams. Furthermore, King Zavaxer will no longer rule us. The Third Order's noble self-sacrifice for our benefit will ensure that certain members of our leadership gain the support necessary to oust him. The Third and First Orders shall then be one and the same. A complicated plan, perhaps, but an elegant one.

* * *

A side note of my own: it can be gathered, I am sure, that my informant is someone of note in Laitmean society. (One more reason for Uncle to destroy this record if we are discovered.)

However, they have been clear that anything that might implicate their own untoward involvement in King Darin's demise can be explained away as the Queen's faulty recollection. I am not so sure. Incriminating evidence is much harder to fully erase than people like to think. Also, I will be interested to see what gems we turn up on Redgenold the elder. He has a most annoying habit of keeping his nose clean.

It is common knowledge that he is considered to be a prince because his father was Queen Elisabet's brother, killed in the fighting that marked the beginning of King Darin's reign. However, it is said that this information was gleaned from letters that were sent to Redgenold's maternal uncle, a Haputian peasant named Efin.

The late war hero and queen's brother clearly wasn't in the habit of corresponding with his son's uncle—especially since he was dead at the time. It can thus be assumed that the letters were written by Redgenold's mother. This is entirely more interesting, as she was a mass murderer. Might explain why he married a mad woman himself.

* * *

VEENA

Mayzin

Mer is sending an envoy to the palace, to express their displeasure with the Queen and my mother. Really, they could have done that with a letter. Father says that they're going to want to negotiate some kind of deal involving Laitmean ships no longer being protected from pirates. They must know that the chances of that succeeding are zero. I wish them luck. My mother has been chasing my father with a poleaxe, and the Queen has hidden throwing knives in her night clothes.

On a lighter note, Bella is successfully married. Her mother is furious of course, but it is far too late to do a thing about it, and my mother chipped in and said that Bella had been to stay and must have run off instead of going home, so I have not taken any of the blame. Mad as she is, mother is still wonderful sometimes.

I am nervous to see Arabell again, though. it's more than likely to happen, as everyone is already discussing holding a ball for the coming diplomat and whatever attendance he brings with him. I'll just act like I'm really pleased to see her, I guess. And like I haven't been writing to her daughter every week.

* * *

To Mayzin:
   You and cousin Benji are the only members of high society that I'm keeping in

touch with. *I'm finding that I like the aristocracy much better this way: at a distance. It's lovely to sit beside the fire and read all the gossip and happenings, without having to take part in any of it. Besides, the two of you are nice enough not to include the gossip that's about me.*

The shine may have worn off, but I'm still happy here. Happier than I ever was in court, whether it be in Lifeth or the capital. Best of all, country women don't tighten their corsets to the point of suffocation. You have no idea how comfortable they are when they fit correctly.

Finny's still as sweet as ever, and we made friends with the young couple down the road: the cobbler and his wife Dezzie. They have three young children and a lovely little farm on Lord Fankherst's land. It's just enough for a horse and some chickens, but they love it dearly and so do I. I'll save the best news for my next letter, when I'm sure of it. (As if you can't guess,)

Yours, Bella.

* * *

Veena

We have been on the road from Pirate's Cove for a week now. I say road, but that is somewhat an overstatement. The dusty track that will shortly bring us through the Aegot Forest is so faint that in places we must make our best guess by compass and stars which way to go. Still, it is more of a road than any of Mer's trade routes that can be found on a map. The path from Djabet to Corris is eroded by the wind each winter, when no merchants dare to travel for the cold.

It is exceedingly dangerous to navigate the Dust Lands, for dust storms often cloud the stars and the price of getting lost there is death by cold or dehydration. Here in the east, we have it a little better. Still, being on the road makes Uncle far more irascible.

* * *

Little of note has transpired during our travels. Now that we are about to enter Lyrah, the capital, I must make note of a few more facets of our deception. King Zavaxer is under the impression that he is the one to have requested a meeting with King Dowlin and Queen Trilliapa.

His correspondence has actually been heavily altered by my Uncle, so the Laitmean nobles are under the impression that he wants war, not peace. Uncle will meet with them, and give them one last opportunity to relinquish their ships without bloodshed. This is largely a front to allow me contact with the younger Redgenold to enact the first stage of our plot.

Henceforth, I shall be known as Violet, the diplomat's dedicated apprentice. Ironic, Uncle says, because I am clearly anything *but* a dedicated apprentice. I think he confuses dedication with attitude. One does not need to be good at one to have the other.

There will be a ball to welcome us the first night of our stay in the capital, because this is Laitmea, and every occasion needs to be marked with a ball or the sun will not rise the next morning. Even if they know as well as I do that we two diplomats do not come in peace, but to lodge complaint.

Well, a ball will serve me very well, I think. I do look stunning in a periwinkle silk dress.

* * *

Jessimin

Jessimin was dozing at the table. It was the first time that she had been allowed to stay for the duration of a party, and she had enjoyed feeling a part of high society, although it would be another three years before she was of age and able to participate fully.

Still, it was now well past the hour when she would have ordinarily been tucked snugly into bed. She found now that she was almost missing the nursery, and the company of her younger cousin Alloysius. Her pale pink dress was beginning to feel itchy and hot, and the heels on her shoes were making her feet ache.

She had eaten more than her fill of pastries, and danced twice with the group. No boys had asked her to dance, and she doubted that she would have been allowed to go if they had. All in all, she thought it had been an excellent party, if a little stuffy.

She knew she should have paid more attention to the politics of the evening, as a princess, but she simply couldn't bring herself to find the diplomat for Mer interesting.

Whatever was going on between her own nation and theirs was a problem for her parents, aunts and uncles. She wasn't going to worry herself over it quite yet. In any event, whatever discussions they were going to have wouldn't begin until the next morning. Now, it was time for frivolity and a few too many desserts.

The ball was still hours shy of wrapping up, so Jessimin took to watching people to pass the time.

Her siblings were, by far, the most interesting attendees to watch. Perhaps only because she knew them so well, and could guess the subject of their conversations without having to be within earshot. Perhaps because they were having the most interesting conversations.

Pippy was dancing with with a young man whom she did not recognize. If she had to guess, she would have said that he was the younger son of someone important. Not an heir to anything, (he seemed far too carefree for that,) but well-dressed enough for her to know that his parents must be incredibly wealthy. She wondered how serious his intentions with Pippy were. She was only a few months shy of sixteen, and he looked to be about seventeen or eighteen.

Jessimin knew that many young couples these days weren't getting married until they had been of age for several years, but she doubted that Pippy would be one of them. She decided that she would need to interrogate this gentleman caller later; if he wasn't a fit match for her sister, someone needed to step in, and it certainly wouldn't be her parents, who were currently staging a mock duel with a serving fork and ladle.

She moved on to watching Kestly, who looked torn between distancing herself from their parents, and joining in the melee. In the end, she settled for leaving the party by way of the window. Jessimin doubted that anyone else had seen her; Kessie was a master at sneaking out of windows. She wondered briefly where her sister was going, then watched Xeno for a while, as he flirted with a dozen different young ladies, all while downing an endless stream of confectioneries. He seemed particularly fond of the peanut flavored ones. She knew he didn't care for any of the nobles daughters, his one true love was a baker's daughter. It made a certain sort of sense, she thought, seeing as his other true love was everything else at the bakery.

Mayzin was a few tables away, happily chatting with a frumpy old Lady whom Jessimin only vaguely recognized. She seemed to recall that this was the mother of one of Mayzin's childhood friends, Bella. If so, this sister was likely being interrogated as to Bella's whereabouts.

Jessimin smiled to herself. If the snippets she had gathered from various conversations and poking through Mayzin's diary were to be believed, Bella had run away with a stable-hand, was now happily married, and was likely expecting her first-born. It wasn't supposed to be common knowledge, but Jessimin thought the old lady was probably the only one who didn't know.

It took her several more minutes to spot Marley, who was hiding in a corner, looking thoroughly overwhelmed. She couldn't blame him. He was the quietest and the sweetest of her brothers, and he had probably had his fill of dancing and carousing within a quarter hour of the ball's start.

He lacked the bad manners necessary for climbing out a window like Kestly, though, so he was employing the age-old tactic of pretending to be a rock. So far, it seemed to be working. No one had asked him to dance, and he was so well hidden that she doubted anyone ever would.

That left only her two oldest siblings, who were least familiar to her. Lara, she knew, had left some hours ago with her husband. They were both nineteen, and though Jessimin liked them a lot, they could be boring. Six out of seven siblings accounted for. She wondered where Redge was. That boy was a magnet for trouble, even more than Kessie was.

Although he was named after their father, he took after their mother to such a startling degree that she often joked that he ought to have been named Pippy, and Pippy, Redge. Twisting around in her seat, Jessimin finally spotted him. He was in the corner opposite Marley, but he was not alone. Standing only inches apart from him was perhaps the most beautiful girl Jessimin had ever seen.

She was wearing a pale, periwinkle blue dress with a full, floaty skirt. It was almost shockingly low cut in the front, and nothing but a lace in the back. Personally, Jessimin thought that it was overkill. Somebody with that much blonde hair didn't need periwinkle lace too. Jessimin knew that her own curls were the envy of many, but they paled in comparison with this young woman's multitudinous braids. The entire ensemble appeared to be held in place with a single ribbon and a real periwinkle trapped inside the glass bulb on a pin.

Jessimin had always loved flowers in glass baubles. She had a similar paper weight on her desk filled with roses from last summer's garden. She watched appreciatively as the lamp-light reflected off of the piece when the girl threw back her head to laugh. So engrossed with the flower, it took Jessimin several seconds to realize that the girl must have been laughing at something that her brother had said.

Immediately, she forgot all about preserved flowers, her ears pricked. Redge the younger was no comic. It was strange enough for him to have attracted someone that pretty, so unless her senses had completely deceived her, there was something strange afoot.

Try though she might, she could not make out more of their conversation, so she casually rose to her feet, stifling a moan as she settled back onto her aggravating heels. She made as if to go to the lavatory, then once in the hall outside, wove her way around the ballroom until she found a large niche approximately level with the spot she had last seen Redge standing.

Trying to make as little noise as possible, she lifted a heavy decorative candelabra out of the niche, kicked off her shoes, and climbed in. She knew that there was no way to construe this as anything other than eavesdropping, and though she spent the least time with Redge of any of her other siblings, she knew that the intrusion would not please him one bit.

This was the most naughty thing she had done in years, and had she been a little less tired, a little less bored, or a little less full of peanut crunch and ice cream, she probably would have thought better of it. As it was, she was absolutely dying to know what her brother was doing with a girl like that.

She leaned her head against the wall, and much to her delight, could clearly make out the sound of her brother's conversation. Her childish enjoyment was short lived, though. She listened with growing horror and a sinking feeling in her over-full stomach.

"Of course, I've thought of being king, as any prince does, even one as far from the throne as me," Redge was saying. "But I couldn't really enact that plan, could I? What you're saying sounds lovely, and I can't pretend that I haven't dreamed of it before, but I don't think that I hold the clout to pull it off."

The young woman laughed again, and Jessimin was startled to hear that her voice was almost as pretty as she was. For some reason, she had expected the pretty girl to talk in a snake's hiss.

"Oh, Redgenold, you'll never be king with an attitude like *that*. What I'm offering, it's only what you deserve. You're a prince for goodness sake, and a far better one then many before you."

What was she offering? Jessimin wondered, alarmed. She'd been a princess her whole life, and had only ever expected to remain one. She and her siblings were heirs in name only; if one of them were to ascend to the throne, it would only be as the result of some unspeakable tragedy. Surely, her brother was not about to make a deal that would result in the deaths not only of the King and Queen and their parents, but all of their cousins as well. She refused to believe it.

"What does your Uncle think about all of this?" Redge asked, from the sound of it standing closer to the wall then he had been. Jessimin hoped that it didn't mean that he was also closer to the girl who ought to sound like a snake.

"My Uncle doesn't know. He's as loyal a pirate as anyone can be, although even that entails *some* treason."

This time, it was Redge who laughed.

"But you're not making a deal with the king."

Jessimin fought the urge to throw up some of her peanuts. She knew who this girl was now: the niece, and apprentice, of the envoy Mer had sent. Violet, one of the people for whom this ball was being held. Of course, everyone knew that the diplomats really came from the pirate king, but they had all hoped that the pair would be a little more civil than this.

"Then who am I making a deal with?" Redge sounded confused.

"Me, silly."

They both laughed. Jessimin moaned, and hopped out of the sconce, putting the candelabra back before she was discovered, or worse, had to listen to more of her brother's disgusting conversation.

It was clear that while he thought he was the one doing the plotting, he was really just a pawn in the pirate Violet's nefarious plot. Mer didn't want Redge on throne, she knew that much. What they could gain by manipulating him,

31

though, she could only guess. He must have been an easy target for a girl like Violet. She didn't see why else the pirates would choose him, as he lacked both brains and charisma.

But that answered the *why*, and not the *what*. What in Eretz could the pirates want with her brother? So far as she knew, their mission was to convince the King and Queen that they should be allowed to attack Laitmean ships, and that the Queen and her own mother ought to stop using their former affiliation with the order to try to influence Mer's politics.

But now this rogue Violet was striking deals with her brother. Had they given up on peace? Were they trying to weaken the country in order to take over? Was Violet really acting independently of her Uncle, or were the pirates as a whole out for blood? And who, if anyone, could she trust with the knowledge of what she had just heard?

She slipped back into her shoes and trotted to the ballroom door. Certainly not her parents, whose cutlery duel had reached epic proportions by the time she reentered the ballroom. Certainly not the King or Queen, either. Both of them had far too much on their plates with the arrival of the envoy, and if Redge was plotting against them, alerting them might only put them in more danger.

Mayzin would be a sympathetic ear, if she were on her own, but she was still contending with Bella's mother. Pippy might have a good idea or two on how to deal with Redge, but she was still dancing. Marley was too shy and avoidant of conflict to want anything to do with her eavesdropping.

Seeing the that room was utterly devoid of help, Jessimin whirled around and marched right out again. Holding back tears, she bolted up flight after flight of stairs, until she reached the palace roof. There, under the moonlight and stars, her aunt's dragon was sleeping.

As she approached, he opened one orange eye, and flicked his tail at a flat section of the crenelated wall. Jessimin sat where he had indicated, and in between great gulps of cool night air, spilled out all of her heart's worries to the enormous green dragon.

Dart was better than any diary. He listened with something approaching sympathy, a certain bright intelligence in his eyes. Although she could never go back and read her words over, she found it comforting to know that they were kept in something far stronger than a locked drawer, which anyone could break into.

No prying eyes could read what she told Dart. He offered her no advice on what to do—he never had and never would. But he sat patiently, showing no inclination to return to his nap until she had collected her thoughts and decided what to do.

When she finally rose to leave, she gave him a gentle scratch behind the ears before descending to the party once more. She hadn't been gone long enough for anyone to be suspicious; indeed Redge was so engrossed in his conversation with Violet that she doubted that he noticed her absence at all.

She still felt nauseous at the thought of what she had heard, and at the thought of peanuts, but she was calm enough now to pretend that nothing was wrong.

It was well past midnight when the party finally dispersed, and everyone was far too tired to notice anything except the soft white covers on their beds. But when the morning sunlight roused them, Pippy and Mayzin would find identical notes slipped under the cracks of their doors.

> *We need to talk. My room, now.*
> —*Jessimin*

* * *

JESSIMIN

Veena

Being Violet has proven useful. No one suspects a delicate blue flower. I have ingratiated myself quite well with the crazed prince. Yes, he is every bit as cunningly mad as his mother, but he is also an eighteen year old man, and thus easy to manipulate.

Last night at the ball, I danced with no one else, nor he with another girl. I told him many things, but none were lies, so there is no need to record them here. Suffice it to say, he is under my control now, as surely as the great green dragon sleeping atop the palace is controlled by the queen. He thinks I want to marry him. Poor boy.

Uncle is meeting with the King and Queen today. I will most likely need to make a long and tedious record of this affair when it is through, so for now I shall rest my writing hand and have a stroll about the city. Who knows whom I may meet by chance.

* * *

Mayzin

I woke this morning to a note from Jessi, saying that we needed to talk. I knew that it had to be something important for her to have stayed up long enough to write me a note last night. She had looked asleep on her feet after the ball.

Sure enough, she called me and Pippy in to her room to tell us that our brother is plotting something. The conversation she recounted with just awful. I won't copy it down just on the off chance that Redge breaks in and reads this.

Of course, I'll kill him if he does that, so I guess there's no harm in saying that Jessi listened in on him plotting to take over all of Laitmea with the pirate girl Violet. There was no one besides Pippy and me that Jessi trusted with the information, which I think is just as well.

Best that not too many people hear of Redge planning treason. The problem is, she didn't really listen in on enough of the conversation for us to know exactly what he's plotting. He always was a strange child though, so I'm sure that it can't be anything innocent.

We need to find out more before we tell anyone of course, so we will be taking a turns trailing him to see if he does anything untoward. Pippy is up first, as she doesn't have any plans for today. Jessi will follow him tomorrow, and will I the day after that. If he manages to behave himself, we will assume that he was only posturing for the attention of the very pretty Violet. However,

36

if he is involved in anything suspicious, we will find out what it is.

* * *

Kanara

Kanara couldn't help but wish that he had several extra bones in his neck to turn his head round on. The trek through Laitmea's forests had been strange enough, with green trees as far as the eye could see and pools of water by which to camp each night. There had been birds and beetles and shy deer in abundance, too. It had been strange and wondrous to see that the world contained so many living things, but Lyrah did not seem to belong to this world at all.

Everywhere, buildings sprouted up, packed closer than the trees had been. Some short, some tall, some wood, some stone. The streets were nothing like the dirt tracks he had followed his entire life, either. They were cobbled with thousands of small flat stones or squares of tile that made the horses' hooves clack.

Strangest of all were the people. There were hundreds, no, thousands of them. Some of the oldest families in the desert had been twice the size of his, and Kanara had found visits to their camps to be crowded, noisy, and confusing. This crowd was so mind-bendingly vast that he gave up trying to make sense of it all, and instead focused on leading the parade of horses through the narrow ways without leaving any small cousins behind.

Even so, every few steps he found his eyes dragged away by some shiny trinket or other, or his ear caught by fragments of some strange voice. He was surprised that he was not attracting more strange looks himself. Then again, the masses pressing in around him possessed every shade of hair from midnight black to a strange rusty sand-like color. Some men even had white hair, thought they were not old at all.

When first Kanara saw this, he turned right around, sure that his eyes had deceived him, but now he marveled that even some children here had white hair, and in greater numbers than adults. There were those too, with eyes like cut crystals, blue and green and gray. He supposed that if one were surrounded by such a wide array of humanity every day, a few dark-haired nomads were hardly worth a raised eyebrow.

They had crossed the bridge over the river Quir and into the city early that morning, and though Kanara had been happy with their progress, he knew that they still had far to go.

"Katjia," he called, and his little sister guided her horse up beside his. "We will need a place to stay the night. Even if fortune smiles upon us greatly, it will still take us several days to conduct our business. We can't afford anything too grand or too far from this market district. Can I trust you to find us accommodations and meet me back here by the time the sun touches the horizon?"

"Of course," she said, and plunged down an alleyway without a backward glance.

He sighed. Katjia was more than capable, but he still worried about her. She was as tight as a coiled spring and at times far harder than he was. She was not old enough to remember the war, but it had shaped her nonetheless. She berated him for being too hesitant and too concerned over other's opinions.

He decided that when she returned, it would be his turn to berate her for being too rash, and not conscious enough of others feelings. She hadn't even paused to wish him farewell before tramping off to find the perfect camp. Infuriating.

* * *

Marley

I have been assigned a rather dull math problem. Normally, I enjoy the subject well enough, but today I am finding it tedious, so I am writing in here instead. Mother and Father have been in the throne room all morning, talking with the diplomats from Mer.

I have to say that the welcome ball held for them last night was not to my liking. If I were the diplomat, I would have turned right around and left, rather than subjecting myself to that long of a party.

I much prefer solitary activities or things I can do with Mayzin. My favorite thing of all is to go to the docks and watch the ships come and go. It's a peaceful place, as long as you stay out of the workers' ways, and I can sit for hours and draw. I have about ten sketchbooks full of drawings. I might sketch some in this book, if I have time. Ships fascinate me, so I mostly do diagrams of rigging and such, but sometimes I draw flowers for Mayzin.

I saw a dragon head on a keel yesterday that had a rose in its mouth. I'm sure that it has gone back down the river now, but I would love to show it to Mayzin. In fact, I would rather be on a dock with her right now.

I would like it more than anything else in the world, so I think I shall pack this book in my satchel and sneak out the window the next time our tutor leaves for the lavatory. I'll see if I can find the dragon head with its rose. Mayzin will probably come with me. She doesn't much like sneaking out of windows, but she likes me.

I don't much like breaking rules either, but it's been even stuffier than usual, with everyone tense over the situation with Mer. High time for a stroll about the city. More later.

* * *

Katjia

Katjia pushed through the crowded market street, leading her horse, Petrushka. She had already passed three inns, each with cheery signs proclaiming the comfort of their beds or the delectable nature of their food. Had any one cost less than a crown per person, she might have considered renting rooms, but they couldn't afford a bed for every aunt and cousin, or even half of them, if it came to that.

She suspected that her brother had assigned her an impossible task. There was not a single green space in the city that was not kept behind high walls and wrought iron fences. Unless they wanted to pitch their tents miles outside, they would need the permission of some lord or noble to spend the night in their private garden.

Katjia was fairly sure that that would be even more expensive than trying to rent rooms. It could take them weeks to buy and sell what they needed to, but their quest would end far sooner if they did not have a place to spend the night. She drew Petrushka to the side as a carriage trundled past and sighed. So many people.

She would have liked to find a quiet spot just then, a place to sit and think about their predicament without distraction. She turned down another side street and, like an answer to her unspoken prayer, saw an empty space at its end.

She trotted forward with more purpose now, and found that the street sloped downhill to open up on the bank of the northern branch of the river Quir. She could see, not a quarter mile to the east, the place where the river's two branches met in a roiling white waterfall. The falls were much broader than they were high, and they protected the main gates into the city. Katjia had heard their dull roar when they had crossed the great southern bridge into Lyrah, but she had yet to see them.

Curious, she made her way down the path along the river bank, passing only a young couple and a harried shopkeeper along the way. She had the river at her left, the backs of buildings at her right, and a blessed moment of solitude. She realized that this was the most alone that she had ever been. In the desert, being on her own would have been frightening. Here, she found it peaceful.

The falls before her blotted out all the noise of the city. She saw that there was a broad stairway beside them, with a high wall on either side. She had wished that she would be able to stand right beside the rushing torrent, but she realized that it probably wouldn't have been safe.

The stairway led down past the outer wall to the docks, which were the hub of trade between Laitmea and Haputa. She knew that beyond the docks, the combined rivers flowed through miles of uninhabited land, past Quirton, and out to the sea. Pirates' Cove was said to be near the mouth of the river, but she had never seen a map that showed its exact location.

She found a post next to the top of the stairs for tying horses, and left Petrushka on a long enough rope to reach the lush grass beside the river. She wondered if there was room enough beside the docks to camp. It would be challenging to move their belongings up and down the stairs, but they would still be close to the heart of the city without being on someone else's land.

She saw a deep groove cut into the wall on her right, fitted with ropes and pulleys, which must have been used to winch heavy goods up and down. There was probably a fee to use the ropes. She moved a little faster, aware that it was now early afternoon. She needed to move more quickly.

After an interminable number of steps, she exited the stairwell and saw the river spread out before her. The base of the falls was a frothing white mound, but after only a few feet the water smoothed into a fast flowing mirror. She counted twenty piers jutting out into the current, each with at last one boat tied to it. Some of the ships were enormous, but most looked as if they could only hold a dozen or so passengers.

There were hard packed dirt paths between each of the piers, bustling with activity. Farther from the riverbank, dozens of buildings were swarming with even more people and, to her delight, horses.

She saw a dozen spots that might be tolerable to make camp in, if they were not being used already. She wondered if there was someone in charge of the whole operation who she could ask. She didn't want to lead her family to a likely spot only to have them driven off by some incoming shipment.

Katjia raised her hand to stop a passing carpenter, but he rushed by her without even seeing it. No luck. Everyone was rushing to and fro as quickly as their legs could carry them, and as she made her way further down the road, she felt that she had been plunged straight back into the heart of the city. Only now it all smelled faintly of fish.

Then, at the far end of the half mile long shipyard, she saw a small cluster of people who weren't moving. Two young women, one about her age and one a few years older, and a boy. Maybe one of them could point her in the right direction.

As she got closer, she saw that all three were dressed very well. The younger girl and boy were wearing particularly fine clothes, and aside from the fact that one was wearing a skirt, and the other pants, they were almost identical. They had gold hair so fine and pale that it almost looked white, pretty round faces, and soft, delicate hands that looked as though they had never held a horse's reins.

The older girl was stunningly beautiful. She too had golden hair, but it was flowing loose over her shoulders. Her large eyes were a deep shade of brown, her lips were cherry red, and her skin was lightly tanned. Katjia had never thought that a foreigner could match the beauty of her people, but this girl could have had songs written about her.

"Excuse me," she said, drawing up beside the strange trio, "could any of you tell me who is in charge here?"

The girls whirled around, looking at her like she was some sort of oddity found lurking under a rock. The boy, who was sitting on an upturned barrel, drawing the scene before him with a piece of charcoal, did not move.

"I want to speak with someone about the greensward between...ah... dry docks nine and ten..." she trailed off, unsure.

"Feroy Kaedric is in charge of the dry docks. But if you're only interested in the dirt between them, you'll want to speak with the shipments manager, Keeralyn Ilkare," the boy said, laying down his half-finished drawing.

"Feroy is usually in the administrative building near the causeway, and Keeralyn is out inspecting a shipment of wool. He won't be back for another hour at least."

"Thank you," Katjia said, wondering why the two girls were still staring at her, and why the boy hadn't even looked at her.

"Where are you from?" the younger girl suddenly blurted, blue eyes wide with curiosity.

"Onkay, miss."

"I've never met anyone from Onkay before," she said, then hastily amended, "except for one diplomat, but I only saw him from a distance. Does everyone there look like you?"

"As much as everyone from Laitmea looks like you, I suppose," Katjia said, nonplussed.

"I'm Mayzin," the girl said, "Princess Mayzin Avilamin Della. What's your name? And how are you finding Lyrah?"

"I'm Katjia, your highness. I had no idea that you were one of the princesses. Are all three of you royalty?" she dropped into a clumsy curtsy, in case it was expected of her.

"That's my twin brother, Prince Marley," Mayzin said, gesturing to the boy, who Katjia supposed to be very handsome, in his own way.

"And this is Violet. She's the niece of Mer's envoy, out enjoying the sights of our capital. There's no need to be so formal with us, though. You couldn't have known that you were speaking to nobility."

Katjia smiled. The princess was clearly within a few months of her own age, and as bright as a new penny.

"I've found the capital quite impressive, if a bit crowded," she said, "I suppose you're showing your guest around?"

"Not at all. Technically speaking, we're not even supposed to be here, hanging around the docks like commoners. But Marley loves to watch the ships, and I didn't want him to get into trouble. Which invariably happens when he sneaks out by himself. He's absolutely useless at avoiding detection."

Violet huffed, and said, "I met them by chance a few minutes ago. Although I'm not supposed to be here either." She tossed her hair over one shoulder in a disdainful manner, and continued in a surprisingly musical voice.

"I find politics boring, so I took the first opportunity I could find to extricate myself from the diplomatic proceedings and go exploring. On my own. Normally, a young lady such as myself would never be permitted to do so, but Mer's diplomat is my Uncle, so I find that I have certain liberties. I don't doubt that my Uncle will fill me in on all of the day's dull details when I return, anyway."

Katjia nodded politely, and congratulated her on her daring escape, but privately she decided that she didn't much like Violet. She looked to be about seventeen, and very haughty. Mayzin had a delightful air of mischief about her, but Violet seemed to think that breaking rules was her right.

They chatted for a while more, about a dozen inane and inconsequential things. Katjia wasn't quite sure how to extricate herself from the conversation. She needed to talk to Keeralyn Ilkare before the sun sank much lower in the sky, and as pleasant as Princess Mayzin was, she wanted to get away from Violet.

Marley eventually spoke. He had returned to his drawing, which she could see now was quite skillfully done.

"What brings you here, Katjia?" he asked.

"Famine." she stated, bluntly.

"Ah, I'd heard that Onkay was teetering on the brink of starvation for some time now. Do you come for provisions, or to stay?"

"My family needs to eat," she said. "For right now, that means buying food, but if we do not soon receive word that the rains have returned, then we may stay for quite some time. That is why I want to speak to Keeralyn Ilkare. We will need a place to pitch our tents, not too far from the city center. Ideally, not for any great cost, either. We do not want to have to sell our horses just yet."

"If your family is very large, you won't fit between the dry docks. Why don't you come and pitch your tents in the rear courtyard of the palace? No one in our family uses it, and it has a goodly amount of shade trees and grass, which I am sure that your horses will like. It's closer to the heart of the city than just about anywhere else. I can also offer it to you free of charge, for the night, at least. After that, you could work things out with Aunty Trill."

"Aunty Trill?"

"Queen Trilliapa."

Katjia gaped at the back of his head, shocked. She had known generous people, but this was more than she ever could have imagined.

"Are you quite sure, Prince Marley? That is very kind of you."

"Yes, I'm sure. You need a place to stay, don't you? Just tell the guards that I invited you."

Mayzin looked like she wanted to say something, but Katjia was already leaving. She didn't want to give them time to change their minds.

"I must go fetch my brother, then! Thank you!" she called over her shoulder.

Maybe not an impossible task after all.

* * *

MAYZIN

MARLEY

Marley

I am sitting at the docks right now, sketching a rather impressive long ship. I am not, however, enjoying the sole company of my sister. We have been interrupted not once, but twice, this fine afternoon by strangers of a most peculiar nature.

First, when we were on our way here, we happened to bump into the niece of Mer's diplomat. It seems unusual that the envoy of a foreign government would cross the country with no one but a young lady. I wonder what her real purpose here is? She obviously knew who we were, and seemed as surprised to see us as we were to see her. Her name is Violet. I suppose she's pretty, but I don't like her much. There's something quite *off* about Violet.

She asked us a lot of questions about our thoughts on Mer and Laitmea's relationship, and whether we thought Aunty Trill and Uncle Dowlin are doing the right thing by keeping the pirates from attacking our ships. Even chatty Mayzin didn't answer that one.

I don't know if it's exactly wise of them to use their old affiliation with the pirates to try to influence Mer's politics, but I'd be a fool if I said so to her.

And I really don't think we ought to let the pirates steal our goods. There's something to be said for private property, especially when it's the only thing keeping this country from starvation. The pirates' way of life just isn't right, whatever they might tell themselves.

I think Violet is one of the pirates, and I'm sure the diplomat is, too. He's the same medic who treated my mother for the plague, all those years ago. I guess I'm grateful to him for that, seeing as I wouldn't exist if mother had died, but it's not a good sign that the pirates are officially showing that they're in charge of Mer.

Anyway, Violet followed us down to the docks, not telling us anything about herself, just asking more and more questions. She's quite good, really. I found myself tempted to answer more than a few. I do have one question of my own, though: What was she doing before she ran into us?

She certainly didn't plan our meeting, though she's taken full advantage of it, so she must have other motives for wandering the city. She says that the diplomat's meetings are boring, but I don't think she'd have been selected to accompany him if she really thought so.

The other stranger we bumped into was more pleasant by far. Her name is Katjia. She came with her family from Onkay, to escape the famines. Onkay is mostly desert to begin with, but the people there have been eking out some kind of living for generations. Recently, however, we have been hearing reports of dry weather. Now, it has become dire enough for even the oldest and richest of the nomad families to seek food elsewhere.

It has been two full years since rain has come to most of the desert, when in the northern reaches, it had fallen once or twice a year for as long as anyone can remember.

Her family was on the brink of starvation when they left, and their fortunes have not much improved. They will be able to trade for what goods they need, for they breed horses finer than any we see in Laitmea, but they had no place to stay.

They want to save their coins for food, not waste them on expensive city lodging, so Katjia was sent to search for a place to pitch the tents they brought. I offered the palace courtyard to them.

Mayzin says it was a fool thing to do, but it's not as if any of us use it. It's just a nice view from cousin Addmaleta's window, but if the rest of the nomads are as pretty as Katjia, it'll still be a nice view.

She's a strange looking girl, with worn out riding clothes made of horse-leather—a scandalously short split skirt and breeches, boots, shirt with no sleeves, and short cloak to keep the sun off. Her hair and eyes and skin are all the same shade of blackish brown, too, which I've never seen before, but it makes her all the prettier.

She had her hair in three long braids, a sort of style that would look nice on Mayzin if she didn't think such things were improper. They say girls in Onkay are trained to keep lions away from the herd with nothing but a staff and strong words. I wonder if it's true?

* * *

Kanara

The sun was hanging low above the rooftops when Katjia returned. She was on foot, leading her horse behind her. Kanara sighed. He had feared that she would get lost, or be unable to find them a place to stay. Her happy trot showed him that his worries were groundless, but still. She was his only sister now.

He shook himself. Now was not the time to think about Gynn.

"What news?" he asked, shifting in his saddle. It was cool here, like midnight, even with the sun still up.

"We can camp in the palace courtyard!" Katjia said.

"For what charge?"

"None. I met one of the young princes, down by the docks. And a princess, and a diplomat from Mer. Such a load of other people, too."

"The prince has offered us his home for no charge? Are you out of your mind? Why would he do that?"

"Because he is generous? Because we need help, whether we like it or not?"

"We need a place to stay, Katjia, not a fairy tale. I thought you had a better head on your shoulders than this."

"My head is just fine. Follow me."

Kanara moaned, and set off after his sister, who was already moving. He motioned to the rest of the family, who took to their steeds with little enthusiasm. They had been riding for too long, and like him, they thought this promise too good to be true.

A quarter of an hour later, they stood in the back of the palace, before the most impressive wrought iron gate Kanara had ever seen. Taller than two horses it was, and guarded by a stony faced man in light armor and billowing blue breeches. He stared at them, seemingly unfazed.

Katjia jumped down from her horse, and greeted the guard, saying "Hello, sir. Prince Marley said that we could use his courtyard to make our evening camp."

The guard's face was only half visible beneath his helmet, but he must have raised an eyebrow. Kanara could hear it in his voice.

"Why would the prince do a thing like that?"

"My question exactly," Kanara said through gritted teeth. Katjia had clearly been deceived and like a fool had led their entire family to disaster.

Then, to everyone's astonishment, a young man sprinted through the courtyard to the gate. He was dressed in the nicest clothes Kanara had ever seen, though sweat was blooming on his chest. He shoved his tousled, faintly golden hair out of his eyes, panting.

"I... saw... you from the window... came as fast as I could."

He unbarred the gate, and pushed it outward, nearly hitting the startled guard, who said, "Prince Marley! What is the meaning of this?"

"They need a place to stay, we have one. No need to make a fuss..."

Kanara watched, still slightly stunned, as his aunts and cousins poured through the open gate, exclaiming appreciatively at the courtyard's size and lovely greensward.

"Nice to see you again, Katjia," the prince said, as Kanara slowly walked his horse in after them. Would wonders never cease?

* * *

Veena

Uncle and I will be leaving the capital tonight. His meeting with the King and Queen was wholly unsuccessful. They were recalcitrant in their insistence that we pirates are nothing but scum, and that we should content ourselves with their scraps. Ironic, given that they once pirated Laitmea's largest ships and brought great plunder to our order.

But, as I have already noted, our mission is largely a ruse. Uncle stormed out of the audience hall in a huff just as I was returning from my stroll, and reported that everything went exactly as he expected, and I don't need to make note of anything on his end. Just as well, because I have a fair bit of my own record keeping to do.

I let my informant know that Redgenold is under my thrall, and I sent a missive to Carsten, the public head of the Third Order, that he will soon be able to plan his coup. I then had the good fortune to bump into two of the younger royal children—though they are almost of age. Prince Marley and Princess Mayzin. From this meeting, I know that public opinion in Laitmea is in our favor. The people agree that we pirates are in the wrong, of course, but more importantly, they think that the King and Queen are using the wrong methods to deal with us. This is excellent news. Our true candidate for the throne will have little opposition once the documents are made public.

Unfortunately, they did seem suspicious of me after a while, and I had to leave before I was able to confirm the best route in and out of the keep. Even if the coup is able to keep Dart the dragon distracted, it will still be exceedingly difficult to break into the most heavenly fortified tower in the palace without insider knowledge. I will need to try another avenue. If worse comes to worst, we can always come up with a plan on the fly.

As I was preparing to return to Uncle, we were joined by another young woman, a nomad from Onkay. Marley invited her family to stay at the palace, which will complicate our departure somewhat, as they are camped in the rear courtyard we had hoped to leave by.

It must be noted that this young prince is sweet and has a far better head on his shoulders than his older brother. He could pose a threat to our operation, as could several of his siblings and cousins. I will have to have them eliminated as soon as possible. I will discuss the particulars with Uncle when we are on the road. We will need to find a way of disposing of them without alerting anyone to the planned coup.

Right now, I must focus on packing quickly. It will be better all around if Laitmea thinks that we want war. They will focus their attentions on their boarders, and things will go smoother in the capital. Besides, it will be easier for me to cultivate my relationship with the young Redgenold from a distance. Love letters and instructions on wreaking destruction will keep him occupied, and leave me free to make my own plans.

* * *

Marley

The dratted guard at the back gate didn't want to let Katjia's family through. He didn't think *Prince Marley* would have invited such a strange-looking family.

Funnily enough, he's served here for several months, so he should know full well what *Prince Marley* would do. And he should know that as long as I'm being civil, Aunty Trill gives me free rein to be as generous as I like. The royal family has to be better than all of those haughty lower nobles who treat the common folk like dung just because they look a little different and don't dress so fine.

I think that guard came from Aunty Ettalara's estate. She sometimes trains up staff for us. I suppose she would want to maintain a sense of propriety, and these nomads would interfere with that. But he doesn't work for her anymore. And it's not as if people in need of charity would go knocking on her door, anyway.

Nothing against Aunty Ettalara, of course, she's just more uptight about life than is strictly good for her. I think some nomads in the courtyard will add a nice spice to life.

* * *

On another note, it sounds like the delegation from Mer was not at all successful. Small wonder. Aunty Trill was never going to let them pirate our ships. I wonder what Violet is planning now?

* * *

Katjia

Katjia looked at Marley gratefully. Although the prince had no reason to do so, he had given her family a place to stay. She wanted to show him her gratitude, but she wasn't quite sure what to say. "Thank you" didn't seem like enough.

"I hope that your family isn't mad at you," she said after a minute.

"They won't be," he assured her. "Nobody really uses this courtyard anyway. I just forgot to tell the guards that there would be someone here, and they didn't think that anyone in my family would have invited someone to camp here."

"Either way," she said, "I'm glad I met you this afternoon." She wanted to say more, but at that moment, her brother called to her, reminding her of the hour. With a hasty wave she returned to help her family set up camp. Marley lingered for a moment more before turning through the palace gate.

"Strange to be sleeping in someone else's home, isn't it," Kanara stated, watching the prince depart. Katjia only shrugged.

Around the campfire that night, talk was mainly of the disagreements between the royal family and Mer. There was also much discussion about what their own family was to do now, for though they had a place to stay, they were still no closer to finding their own way in the world without the charity of others.

Katjia knew that it vexed her brother to rely on the prince for even this most basic shelter, however, there was no denying that they would be utterly lost without it. The world outside the desert was far more complicated than she could have ever imagined.

Upon setting out she had thought it would be a matter of working and trading for food, and waiting for word that the rains had returned and the famine had come to an end. But the capital was not an inviting place for her tribe, no matter Marley's kindness. She wondered if any of the work they could do or the trades they could be employed in would be of value here.

If the famines outlasted the good grace of the royal family, they might be forced to sell their horses for food, and although the beasts would fetch a substantial price at market, enough to keep them fed for generations, their loss would mean an end to their way of life. Katjia didn't know if she could bear the thought of never returning to the desert.

All these thoughts and more swirled within her mind as she ate her dinner, and listened to her aunts debate whether the pirates of Mer were justified in their demands. She fell asleep looking at the stars through a chink in the branches of the courtyard's flowering trees, and listening to the gentle crackle of their fire as it burned itself out on the cobblestones.

* * *

At first, Katjia thought that the cold night air was what had woken her. Though it was spring, Laitmea was still far more chilly then the desert. However, she soon realized that there were strangers in the courtyard.

After Marley's assurances that no one actually used the space, she was immediately suspicious. It was possible that these were just some members of his family that she had not yet met, but she did not think that the prince was a liar.

No one else in her family seemed bothered by the two shadowy figures making their way along the wall towards the outer parapet, but then, she had always been the lightest sleeper. She watched as the pair silently exited through the gate, wondering if their presence was somehow significant or if she should follow them.

She knew they must have noticed the horses picketed by the entrance, even if they had somehow missed the encampment of nomads by the light of the dying fire. She got up, careful not to wake any of her small cousins, and watched as they both mounted horses, which had been stationed outside. The animals must have been brought there sometime in the night, for she didn't recognize them.

The figures were muffled in cloaks, but she could tell that one was a man and the other a young woman, perhaps even young enough to be his daughter. The woman seemed vaguely familiar, and Katjia debated calling out, but she lost her nerve and decided that it would be best to return to her blankets and let these mysterious people ride away under the light of the crescent moon.

She turned to head back towards her family's encampment, and had to stifle a scream. Marley was standing directly behind her, his shadowed face barely recognizable. He put a finger to his lips, and pointed at the two receding horses. Katjia raised an eyebrow.

In a whisper, the prince said, "That's Mer's diplomat and his niece."

"What are they sneaking away for?" Katjia asked. "I heard that they weren't able to come to a peaceful agreement, but was it really bad enough for cloak-and-dagger operations in the night?"

"I don't think they're afraid," said Marley, "I think they want to get away because it's become clear that the King and Queen won't be giving in to their demands. They aren't interested in any sort of compromise, so they want to get out before their lack of agreement means war."

"So we should let them go?" Katjia asked.

"I didn't follow them to see them safely on their way," Marley said. "The diplomat's niece is Violet. When we met this afternoon, I didn't think much of it, but she might have been up to something. Now that they're running away, I'm even more sure. They might well be going to tell the pirates that there's no deal and they should attack."

"So will you tell the guards to follow them?" Katjia inquired, though she suspected that there wasn't time.

"I don't know," Marley murmured. "I was hoping that I would be able to follow them and actually have something to report when I returned, but I clearly can't keep up with their horses. The only thing I can say for certain is that they left in the dead of night, which is unusual, but not really cause for concern."

Katjia thought for a moment.

"But if there's some kind of trouble, and the pirates come here, my whole family could be in danger!"

Marley nodded. "My thinking exactly."

"I don't like this all," Katjia said, "and I'm not sure how wise it is to follow them, but I think we can keep up with them on horseback."

"We?" asked Marley, speaking above a whisper for the first time, and then looking around wildly as if someone might overhear.

"Of course," Katjia snapped, already running to grab her saddlebags and pack. "Violet rubbed me the wrong way too, and if there's something afoot that might affect both of our families, we need to act now. Since there isn't time to rouse the guards, we can ride after them on my horse. She's quite conveniently picketed by that apple tree."

Marley ran after her, once again whispering. "I've never ridden a horse," he hissed, "and what will we do if we're spotted?"

"Petrushka is a doll to ride, and if we catch up to them, we will tell them that it is an insult to your family's hospitality to be sneaking away without breakfast for the road."

Marley didn't look so sure, but he followed her to the apple tree where the horse was picketed. Katjia had Petrushka sniff his hand, and then hastily hoisted him into the saddle. They rode out of the courtyard only a few minutes behind Mer's diplomat and the strange young Lady Violet.

Katjia had paused only to throw her bedroll on top of her pack and wrap her cloak around her shoulders before jumping up in front of Marley, and the cool night air whipped at their faces as she prodded Petrushka into a gallop. They rode through the twisting streets of the capital, now empty, with all the shops closed and all the inhabitants abed. The silvery moonlight made it a flat, almost desolate landscape, disquieting to Katjia, different as it was from her wide and open desert home.

Their quarry had begun to ride at full speed as soon as they were out of sight

61

of the palace, and though Katjia knew that her horse could easily outpace them even with two in her saddle, she hung slightly back so that their presence would not be detected. They soon rode over the northern bridge that led out of the city, and wound their way into the rolling hills of the countryside.

As the night wore on, neither she nor Marley suggested that they stop their pursuit. It occurred to both of them the diplomat might only have wanted to escape the capital without scrutiny, yet every time one of them thought to voice the idea, the memory of Violet and her strangely probing questions would intrude. No matter what the reason for the diplomat's flight, it seemed most prudent to keep both within their sights.

Marley bounced behind Katjia, barely keeping his hold on her, and she realized that he had spoken the truth about never having ridden a horse. She wondered how he ever could have survived without such a basic skill.

The night was waning, and faint glow was beginning to show on the eastern horizon, when Petrushka cantered to a sudden stop.

"Why did you stop?" Marley asked, his voice barely a croak.

"I didn't," Katjia said, watching the two horses ahead of them bound further up the hill on which they stood.

"Petrushka stopped on her own, which means there must be some kind of danger ahead. She's a strong horse, and smart too, so we can be sure that it's not nothing." The prince nodded, and she felt his chin dig into her shoulder.

There was a stand of trees ahead of them, and with a start, she realized that they must have reached the edge of the Aegot Forest, a startling distance to have traveled in one night; perhaps a sign of their quarries' desperation?

She carefully guided a nickering Petrushka into the shadow of the trees, where they could just make out the diplomats. The horse hid in a pool of shadows, seeming to understand exactly what she intended. Just as she was beginning to think that her intuition was wrong, the early morning silence was shattered by a scream. Bandits were leaping from the trees onto the faint dirt road below.

"We have to help them," Marley shouted,

"The diplomats or the bandits?" Katjia asked. "Either way it's suicide."

In the dim light, flashing knives were all that was visible. Still, it seemed inconceivable that the two riders would survive, as their attackers outnumbered them five to one. The desperate sounds of fighting were spooking the usually calm Petrushka.

Then, to her horror, Katjia felt Marley slither down from the saddle behind her.

* * *

Mayzin

My insufferable brother has invited an entire family of nomads from Onkay to stay at the palace. What was he thinking!

He wasn't. That's the only explanation. His head was full of ships and sailing and he didn't think at all before offering. Sure, the palace is big, but so are families from Onkay. They'll probably come with aunts and uncles enough to turn us all out.

Marley needs to learn about generosity. Namely, there is such a thing as too much of it. You can't help everyone you meet; there simply isn't enough time or money. He is far too nice for his own good. If a bandit stole all his gold, Marley would turn around and offer his horse too.

* * *

Marley is gone! Vanished! I was going to have a talk with him about the tribe camped out in our courtyard, and I can't find him anywhere. I'm going to find Pippy, maybe. She can sort this out.

Xeno's gone too, now that I think of it, probably off cavorting with the baker's daughter. Honestly, this family of mine! Maybe Marley's off with that Katjia, the nomad girl whose family he brought here.

* * *

Katjia

If Marley's horseback riding skills were anything to judge by, he would be nothing but a liability in the fight ahead of them. Katjia knew that she would not be looked upon with kindness if she allowed the prince to be killed, so she hurriedly dismounted.

Her staff was tied behind the saddle. She wrenched it free and, grasping it firmly with both hands, rushed into the fight. Even though she had lead a much rougher life than Marley, nothing could have prepared her for melee combat. Her rudimentary skills with the staff were born out of a need to defend the horses she raised from wildcats.

She reminded herself that her people's fighting skills were well renowned, and prides of lions usually learned that hunting horses was not worth the price. Only lone males, either so large or so desperate that they were willing to risk the staff would dare come near her. So this fight should be easy.

In the gloom, it was easy to pretend that the bandits knives were gleaming teeth, but that I didn't make it any better. She had never tried to fight five cats at once. Still, she threw herself into the fray with a wild abandon, her only goal to protect Marley.

Soon, she was able to crack three of the bandits over the heads, two at the same time with opposite ends of the staff. Marley, who had started off with nothing but his insolently curled fists, grabbed one of their fallen knives and backed himself against a tree.

His pale face was a mask of fear now, and Katjia saw that he had the good sense not to move from his position; he only jabbed the knife at anyone who came too close.

Then, as she moved to stand beside him, Katjia received a small cut on her arm. It was not a life-threatening wound, but the bandit's knife bruised her arm through her thick sleeve. The pain made the already chaotic struggle utterly disorienting, and everything after was a darkness and confusion.

She could no longer see Marley or the diplomats. There were only the seven remaining bandits, closing in on her, intent on killing her. In desperation she prepared to lash out with her staff, backing herself against tree, wondering if anyone would remember her when she was gone.

Surely, battling to the death seven against one was a heroic way to die, but she didn't feel like much of a hero, not knowing what had happened to the prince.

Just as she was beginning to think that all was lost, a woman's voice rang out over the fighting, "Stop! It's over!"

Immediately, the bandits stood down and sheathed their blades. Katjia lowered her staff, unsure. To her surprise, only one more prone figure lay on the ground besides the three bandits she had stunned.

Marley was unharmed and hanging onto a low tree branch above the scene of destruction. Early morning sunshine, just beginning to filter through the tree leaves, illuminated his blond hair and blood streaked, terrified expression.

The bandits she had struck were already regaining their senses, moaning, groaning, and checking to see where their weapons were at.

Evidently, Violet had called for an end to the hostilities. She strode forth from between two trees, appearing unharmed, if unusually disheveled.

Katjia was shocked to see her help one of the bandits to his feet. As she watched, the man removed the cloth mask that had been covering the lower half of his face, and threw back the dark cowl of his cloak.

He was a tall, lanky man, with walnut colored skin and dancing gray eyes. His hair was short but messy, brown with streaks of chestnut and gold, and with a few ribbons braided in around his face.

He could have been any highway robber, but the more Katjia thought about it, the more strange it seemed that the diplomats would be apprehended on such a small and sparsely traveled road. Her suspicions were confirmed when he drew Violet closer, and kissed the top of her head.

Marley did not seem to have drawn the same conclusions she had, for the bandit's actions so utterly shocked him that he fell from the tree with an audible thump.

Everyone, including Katjia, whipped around to stare at him. He winced, standing gingerly. Violet looked from him to Katjia and back again, then said

"Search the area! There may be more of them, and we can't have any witnesses."

"Witnesses to what?" Marley asked. "We only wanted you to be safe."

Katjia groaned as one of the other men lead Petrushka out of the trees.

"Witnesses to my uncle's murder," Violet said, and it was true.

The diplomat's broken body was lying by the roots of a large pine tree. There were dark stains on his clothing, and the hilt of a knife protruding from his chest.

The young man holding Violet spoke, "There was no murder here, just an unfortunate accident. This man and his niece were waylaid by robbers, and when they refused to give up their valuables, they were hard-pressed to escape with their lives."

Violet nodded, crouching beside her uncle's body and rifling through his cloak. She took a small bag of coins, a map, and a thick stack of papers from among his belongings, all while saying, "And if you don't wish to suffer the same fate, that is the only story you will tell."

"And why would we be telling any story?" Marley asked, causing Katjia cringe.

"Because you are coming with us," Violet snapped. "We can't have you returning to Laitmea and telling anyone who will listen that we pirates have troubles among ourselves."

Katjia could see that Marley wanted to protest, but he had the good sense to keep his mouth shut. She herself wanted to ask a number of questions, but she was well aware that most of the men surrounding them still had knives.

She almost spoke out when Violet tied Petrushka behind the other horses, but she knew that it would be better to be dragged along than to be killed on the spot. The knot the pirate tied would never hold a stocky desert horse; Petrushka would likely slip free within a mile, and lose herself in their dense piney surroundings. Katjia hated the thought of anything happening to her, but she was sure that it would be better than being taken by pirates. She only wished that they would be as foolish with her bindings.

Caught up in worry over her horse, it was only belatedly that Katjia realized Marley, as a prince of Laitmea, could be a prime hostage if they were intent on manipulating the King and Queen. She hoped whatever protection his status afforded him would also be granted to her.

Violet ordered them both bound and gagged and hoisted back onto the horse. As the men were tying them up, Violet gestured to the one without his mask and hood.

"This is Carsten," she said conversationally, as if he was a friend and not someone obeying orders to take them prisoner. "He and I are... close."

Katjia suspected that they were more than that.

"We both work for the king of the pirates, who you will shortly have the pleasure of meeting, seeing as you were so inconsiderate as to follow us. We had to have my uncle killed because he was no longer loyal to the king. He was working to create a separate group of pirates, called the Third Order, who aim to start a war with Laitmea. "The King was unaware of the disastrous nature of his diplomatic mission; he was supposed to bargain for peace."

She studied the diplomat's corpse with a calculated expression for a moment before mounting her own horse and leading them deeper into the forest.

"Although," she added, "I had my own reasons for wanting him dead as well."

* * *

Kanara

Kanara bolted awake, scrabbling at the cobblestones, twisting under his blankets. The day was just beginning, the finest thread of golden sunlight shining through the courtyard gate. The air was cool, but not unpleasantly so, and around him, his family was stirring sleepily.

Why then, was he suddenly terrified? Not a thing was out of place. He counted the horses, standing in a row against the back wall in an attempt to lull himself back to sleep. There was nothing to fear. He should rest for another hour, then go back to the market to begin trading.

The second time he counted down the row of horses, it struck him: There was one missing. He counted again. Thirty-three.

He jumped up, running to the empty spot. Had one of the ropes been left too loose? Which one was missing? He counted for a fourth time, and swore at the top of his lungs. Instantly, half of his cousins were awake. He turned around, tugging on his braided hair as hard as he could, aware that a dozen small children were staring at him, wide eyed.

"Congratulations. You just learned a new word," he said, then under his breath added, "and your mothers are going to kill me."

They didn't move.

"Now, which one of you has seen Katjia?"

They murmured among themselves for a few minutes, then the smallest of the bunch, Tio, raised his hand, shaking.

"I was sleeping next to her…" he whispered, "and she got up in the night and took her horse and left. With Prince Marley."

"How would you all like to learn some more bad words?" Kanara asked, letting go of his hair. His cousins nodded enthusiastically.

* * *

KANARA

Marley

I don't even know where to begin this time. When last I wrote, I had just gone out to see if Katjia was settled, and told the guard that her tribe was here at my invitation. I thought that I would complete my next entry after a good night's sleep and a leisurely breakfast—speaking of which, I haven't yet had breakfast. I doubt that I'm going to get it, either—but back to my narrative.

It was near midnight when I remembered that I had forgotten to put this diary back in my bag after the trip to the docks. I put my trousers and shirt back on and went out to retrieve it. I was on my way back to my room when I saw a strange sight indeed: the diplomat and his niece Violet leaving.

They were hurrying through the halls as quiet as frightened rabbits, all of their belongings packed on their backs. I realized that they must have decided that the failure of their talks was cause enough for war.

I followed them, intent on finding out what their next move would be. If they were leaving to alert the rest of their order to attack us, I wanted to be able to provide advance warning. If their motives were something more sinister, as indeed they turned out to be, I wanted to know that too.

I followed them from a distance out of the palace's back gate, and it was there that I came upon Katjia, also awake and watching their progress. When they mounted their horses and fled into the countryside, I thought I would be left far behind, but Katjia dragged me up onto her horse, and we pounded after them with all the speed we could manage. Even with two passengers, her horse was faster than theirs, so we had nearly caught up with them when we reached the forest.

Then, things took a decided turn for the worse. What seemed to be a large posse of bandits fell from the trees and attacked the pair with no shortage of ferocity and knives. I immediately rushed in to help—I've no love for Violet, but I thought that it would be bad form for both members of Mer's delegation to be killed within Laitmean boarders, even if they were sneaking away in the dead of night.

However, I found that knife fights are not the easy, entertaining pastime that my mother would make them out to be. Everything was dark and confusing and utterly terrifying. I nearly got stabbed, and since I had no armor and no means of escape, I climbed the nearest bandit-free tree and hid while Katjia sorted out my mess.

She turned out to be a quite adept warrior, throwing back several of the assailants with he walking staff. I suspect that the women of Onkay do battle lions, and win, if it comes to it.

Then Violet, of all people, called a stop to the proceedings. The bandits were actually other pirates who had conspired with her to kill her Uncle. Their leader, a man by the name of Carsten, is her suitor.

Perhaps they wanted the man off their backs just so they could get married, if he didn't approve of the match, but I think something much worse may be afoot, seeing as Violet revealed that her real name is Veena.

Veena then took Katjia and myself prisoner, charging us to never tell another soul what we had witnessed, upon pain of death. All in all, a harrowing experience. We are now resting in the shade of the trees, waiting to cross the dust lands until the sun goes down. This will make it a frightfully cold and miserable experience, but Veena seems fond of misery. I must say, I don't like her one bit.

I hope she doesn't notice that Katjia's horse got loose and ran off a ways back in the woods. It would probably make her unhappy to lose such a fine animal, and anything that makes Violet unhappy can only make things worse for Katjia and me.

This whole predicament is more than I can handle at the moment. I'm just glad they didn't tie my hands together like they did Katjia's. I'd be quite a sight if I couldn't write or draw in this book.

* * *

Mayzin

Well, my fool of a twin brother is still missing, and he definitely left with Katjia. Her brother came into the palace this morning, asking if anyone knew where they went. To make matters worse, the diplomat and Violet are gone, too.

By now, word will have gotten to everyone her in Lyrah that the meeting did not go well, and in a couple of days, everyone in Pirate's Cove will know too. Either Violet kidnapped Marley and the nomad girl, or the nomad kidnapped him, or something equally disastrous.

I'd say that Katjia and Marley eloped, but however exotic and pretty Katjia might be, Marley's not the sort to do that. If he loves someone, he'll spend a couple of hours telling them about ships, not whisk them away on horseback. I only hope that whoever kidnapped him will return him soon. I miss him already.

It's probably just as well that he's annoying; it'll make the ransom cheaper. He's too sweet for anyone to kill him, either.

* * *

In all the confusion this morning, I almost forgot about Redge. Maybe he arranged Marley's disappearance!

I've been following him since breakfast, and he's not done anything to indicate he knows where Marley is. Still, I agree with Jessi. He's plotting something. We need evidence, and quickly. If anyone would actually hurt Marley, it would be Redge. If Jessi doesn't see anything suspicious when she follows him tomorrow, we'll need a new plan.

* * *

Marley

We were presented to the pirate king, Zavaxer, as incidental hostages. Veena told him that the assailants who slew her uncle were nothing but common bandits. Neither Katjia nor myself said anything to confirm or deny her statements.

It seems that among their order, Veena is significantly more high-ranking than her love, for she ordered Carsten to to watch us.

Apparently, he and his group of miscreants did not break for the day, but rode through the dust lands ahead of us and returned to Pirate's Cove well before they would be missed, or associated with a certain medic's demise. Only a swiftly rotting corpse on the floor of the Aegot Forest is left to tell the truth.

Anyway, King Zavaxer was none too pleased with Veena for capturing us. Again, something is not quite right, for—from what the erstwhile diplomat said—I would have guessed that their king would be happy beyond words to have an actual member of the royal family under his control. But King Zavaxer is not the warmonger that his messages would make him out to be.

* * *

Jessimin

Jessimin paced back and forth, chewing on a loose curl of hair. It was her turn to follow Redgenold, and so far it was turning out to be a disaster.

Pippy had seen him speaking with Violet the evening after the ball, but she hadn't been able to get close enough to overhear any of their conversation.

Piecing together what she had heard from Mayzin, Jessimin guessed that Violet had found Redge after her return from the docks, and before she had barricaded herself in her uncle's room for the remainder of the day. Perhaps there was a reason for this, perhaps not. Perhaps Violet was only bemoaning the large tribe of Onkay's Horse-Lords camped beneath her window. Either way, sometime in the dead of night, she, her uncle, Marley, and one nomad girl had left without a trace.

Mayzin thought that her twin had been kidnapped, but privately, Jessimin thought that a kidnapper wouldn't give him the chance to grab his boots, coat, and diary on the way out. Still, Redge or Violet might be involved.

Pippy had had no reason to suspect that Redge left his room during the night, and the following morning, Mayzin had taken up the watch, albeit after several hours of frantic searching for Marley. She and Pippy had both reported back to Jessimin's room after dark, but they couldn't thrash an ounce of meaning from their observations thus far.

Now, Redge had holed himself up in his room and showed no signs of budging. It was entirely inconvenient. If he had to do something suspicious enough to be followed, the least he could have done was be *interesting* to follow. As the hours crept by, Jessimin began to wonder if she had imagined the entire treasonous conversation. Maybe she had dozed off at the table and had a terrible and realistic nightmare. Maybe this exercise was pointless, and she could stop pacing outside her brother's door and go back to her lessons.

Then she remembered Dart's calm orange eyes, fixed on her as she told him what had happened. She could never have dreamed that, nor could she have dreamed the dragon's interest every time she had given him an update on the situation.

She also couldn't dream of a lesson that would be preferable to this, come to think of it. Her governess had been adamant that she memorize the name of every king of Styllyg, and the name of every soldier in the group that killed the last king, and the name of every prime minister since. Redge was definitely up to something, if only so she could avoid the task with a clear conscience. She wouldn't get in trouble for wasting her day if she came back with real proof of an evil plot against her whole family. She hoped.

Still, she wasn't enjoying pacing back and forth, and she didn't want to stop moving, in case Redge decided to open his door. There were excuses aplenty for walking by, but she hadn't sat outside any of her siblings' doors for years, and she wanted to at least be less suspicious than he was.

Then a thought struck her. His door wasn't the only way into his room. Suddenly excited, she bolted down the hall, glad to be wearing practical shoes for once. She tromped downstairs, out a side door, and through a courtyard full of empty tents and one old lady tending to a row of horses.

She waved and skipped through the flowerbeds around the west wing of the palace. There, at the corner, was a truly impressive growth of ivy. It didn't extend all the way to Redge's window, but it would get her onto the correct ledge.

Heaving herself up, Jessimin resolved to thank whoever planted ivy in such convenient places. It was almost as if all gardeners possessed a sixth sense for where spying might be required.

Jessimin made good time up to the third floor, and slowly edged down toward Redge's room. It was not the first time she had climbed up an ivy-covered wall, but it was the first time she had gone so far along the outside of the palace. The window ledge she perched on was more than wide enough to be safe, and the ivy was close enough to grab at a moment's notice, but the drop was still terrifying.

She wondered how Dart managed to fly. If she were a dragon, she was sure that she'd stay put on the ground. Then she arrived, and peered into her brother's room. The curtains were only half drawn, to keep the sun out. Jessimin breathed a sigh of relief. She had been afraid that he would be keeping them fully closed, to hide his treasonous behavior. But why would he have any reason to suspect that someone was looking in through the window, when he was so high up and so far away from any trees? As it was, there was a good sized chink to look through without being seen. She took a deep breath and looked.

Redge was bent over his desk, scribbling a letter. She couldn't make out his cramped handwriting from her position, but she could see that he was responding to a large stack of mail. That was odd. Who would be writing to Redge? Violet?

He folded the letter, then rang the bell-pull beside his desk. She wished that he would move the stack of letters to the other side of his desk, so she could read the one on top. Instead, he took the lot and crumpled them into a wad. He stood, stretching, and moved to the opposite wall. There was nothing particularly interesting there, just a few landscape paintings and a portrait of him from when he had been a small child.

He gazed at the paintings for a moment, then pulled back the floor grate that led to the furnace system in the bowels of the palace.

The furnace system was a newfangled invention of her father's, which allowed hot air from the great black stove in the basement to rise through the rest of the palace and keep them all comfortable even in the coldest months of winter. It was also an excellent way of dealing with incriminating evidence.

Jessimin watched as Redgenold threw his wad of crushed correspondence down the vent. She remembered her father cautioning her against dropping things down there, the day the enormous pipes had been installed. "Anything that can fit through the pipes will fall all the way down to the furnace and be incinerated instantly. Don't put anything small or valuable too near the grate, and for goodness sake, don't pull the grate up. It might make your room toasty, but it'll more than toast your hands."

Jessimin had never really heeded the warning. The furnace was far safer than having a fire in every fireplace. Nobody's skirt had caught on fire, nor had anyone sprained their back hauling wood up the stairs—for five whole years.

Jessimin knew that father had only been keen on the idea of central heating because the upper levels of the palace had once burned almost completely, taking the lives of three people and a dog. Everyone suspected that the late King Darin had been responsible for the incident, but Redgenold the elder had thought that it was unsafe for the palace to be so easily lit on fire, on purpose or not.

Now she realized that this marvelous invention was dangerous for a whole different reason. She might have combed through fireplace ashes to find out what her brother was up to. Furnace ashes were another matter altogether. She had seen enough.

Jessimin crawled her way back to the ivy, thinking. Rather than return to the ground, she climbed up farther, past the fourth and fifth floors to the roof. Her scaly diary was waiting for her, sunning himself on the hard-baked roof tiles.

"Dart, we have a problem!" she said, rubbing his nose. Dart made a contented grumbling noise, settling in to listen to her story.

"I'm going to tell Pippy and Mayzin what I saw, but I don't know what we can do about it. That furnace burns even hotter than your spit."

Dart growled.

"Well, maybe not that hot, but pretty close. There's no way of knowing what was in those letters. Thanks for the talk, anyway." She left down the stairs, still wondering what her brother could be writing.

* * *

Marley

They've taken everything but my diary. I suppose they think that I won't be able to do much harm with it. Personally, I agree with them. Anyone who says that the pen is mightier than the sword has clearly never been captured by pirates.

Katjia's been disarmed as well, with was a much more impressive feat for our captors. I think they would let her join their ranks if she were amenable, as she's proved herself more than handy in a fight. However, seeing as she's done nothing but curse our captors and all their ancestors' graves, it seems that she is a prisoner now.

I respect her willingness to stand up for what she thinks is right. It takes some strength to hurl insults at people who could easily have you drowned if they felt like it. She's sweet enough towards me, but she makes me very nervous. Sharing a cell with her is interesting, to say the least.

The king, Zavaxer, has made it clear that he doesn't want to risk angering the royal family by killing me, and for the time being, Katjia is extended the same protection. I almost told him that my family wouldn't really miss me, but then I remembered that Katjia would probably kill me for saying that, even if the pirates didn't.

* * *

PIRATE SHIP

Mayzin

Jessimin was the first one of us to see Redge do anything interesting. He's burning his letters in the furnace. That means that there must be something in them that he doesn't want anyone to know, or he would have thrown them in the trash like a normal person. Marley is still missing. We've told mother and father, and Aunty Trill and Uncle Dowlin, but nobody knows what to do.

Father sent out guards to search, but they've found not one trace. It's maddening, sitting here, not being able to do anything, while Marley is off who knows where, probably kidnapped by pirates. The nomads in the courtyard aren't any happier. Their leader, Kanara, is still looking for his sister, too. At least they have a place to stay, and they're able to trade things they've made for the food they need. They make cheese from horse milk that smells abominable, but Pippy actually tried some and says it's quite good.

They've turned out to be exemplary guests. We've even invited some of them in to see the palace. They found all of the towers impressive, but some of the smaller ones were terrified of how high up we all live. I suppose if you've spent your whole life in a tent, it would be a little scary. Whatever I said about Marley at the time, he did the right thing by inviting them. It's been interesting, and the tutors have even let us take time off to sit in the camp. They say it's beneficial to learn about other cultures firsthand. Maybe it is, maybe it isn't, but I'll take a day off from mathematics and politics any time.

Prince Alloysius has made friends with all of Kanara and Katjia's young cousins. Prince Nikolous was actually serious about learning everything to do with their culture. Princess Addmaleta hasn't come out to see them. She's been searching high and low for a bracelet she lost, and is more than a little distraught. It was very valuable, and she kept it in a locked box in her desk.

I think she suspected the nomads of stealing it for a while, but her brothers assured her that they wouldn't do anything of the sort. I agree. Even if they didn't value honesty and integrity so much in the desert, I doubt any of them would dare steal a bracelet from the woman who'll be Queen of Laitmea someday.

If anything, it reeks of Redge. Pippy and Jessi and I have talked in circles all day about what to do.

* * *

Pippy finally had an idea that might just work: turning the furnace off. It's nearly summer, so no one should miss it for a day, and then we can collect any letters Redge disposes of for that day. Of course, there's about a million ways that this could go wrong, but it's the first thing any of us has come up with.

We're all worried sick about Marley and Redge and Violet, and we don't want to be sitting idly by and hoping that father's guards are able to sort it all out.

They don't even know that they should be investigating Redge to begin with, and it would be pointless to tell them when we don't have proof. It would only put him onto us, and the longer he's ignorant of the fact that we know something, the better. So Jessi is going to turn the furnace off tomorrow, and hope for the best.

* * *

Veena

It has been quite some time since I have written in this record. The reason for this is twofold: There were some ugly bloodstains on my entries from the road and several pages needed to be recopied. Also, Uncle really did have a good hiding spot for the first half of this, and it took me nearly a week in his room to find it.

Now that I have some time to continue this account, I have quite a bit of explaining to do. Firstly, I suppose I should say that the plan with the younger Redgenold is still moving ahead, and my informant is very pleased with my progress. I have convinced him fully that he ought to be king, and he is in the midst of planning his coup. There has been only one modification to the plan, and that is that my Uncle is no longer a part of it.

Now this is the hairy bit of the explanation. My Uncle hand picked Carsten to lead the Third Order's rebellion, but Carsten never really worked for him. We had always been partial to each other, and when I was fifteen and he eighteen, we began to see each other in secret. It took me some time to be sure of him, but I eventually shared my deepest secrets with Carsten, and won him away from my Uncle's loyalty.

You see, as I wrote in my very first entry, my Uncle was the best medic in all of Eretz. There were few ailments that were ever beyond his ability to treat. When my father ran away into the Laitmean countryside, my Uncle could have let him go, but he instead remained loyal to the then king, Leopold, and reported his whereabouts. When my parents were captured, he had no choice but to watch my father be put to death.

I do not mourn for my father. He betrayed the order, trapped us in a treaty we had no wish to partake in, and deserved to suffer just punishment for his acts. However, my mother had nothing to do with his treason. She was spared for this reason and because of me.

She was given the choice to join the pirates or give me up to the Second Order when I was born, and she indicated that she might join to be with me. She was under my Uncle's care for the duration of her pregnancy, and, had she lived, I could have been raised by my own parent.

My Uncle claimed that the complications she suffered were unavoidable, and that no one could have saved her. He said that it took all of his skill just to keep me alive, and that my mother bled out and died in his arms only an hour after my arrival. But I always saw a hint of a lie in his eyes when he talked about it.

He thought he could hide it from me, but I saw through him when I was a small child. He didn't save my mother, not because he wasn't able, but because he didn't want to. It would have been a simple matter for him to give her the herbs that could have stopped her from fading away, but he didn't want to. I was enough of a reminder of being betrayed by his own brother. He didn't want another one, living in his own house. I believe that the only reason he didn't kill me too was because he couldn't live with the death of an infant on his conscience.

Carsten later confirmed what I had known all along. When not in my company, Uncle made it quite clear that he *allowed* my mother to die. Thus, as soon as I was able, I wanted to return the favor. Not only were his actions unjust; he deprived me of the opportunity to know my mother. Carsten and I concocted our own plan for vengeance the day we got the news that my Uncle and I were selected to represent Mer to the King and Queen of Laitmea.

Obviously, I couldn't include it in the account my Uncle was having me write, but, for all his flaws, he was correct in thinking that writing things down would be helpful for me.

So I will now say that Carsten took a handful of men of the the Third Order whom he knew he could trust and stationed them along the road through the Aegot Forest. When Uncle and I rode through, the night we left the palace, they fell upon us, and in the darkness and confusion, my Uncle was slain.

It was satisfying beyond words to see the author of my tragic story bleeding out himself, wordlessly, on the bed of pine needles. The ones who did it were low-ranking in the Third Order, and did not know that my Uncle was in charge. They took orders only from Carsten, and thought they were taking an opportunity to remove a prominent member of the King's council.

Carsten then took them back well ahead of me, and did not let on that he knew what had happened. If the men he used become suspicious, or suspect that they inadvertently aided in a coup within their own order, we can always kill them. Carsten assures me that they are all rather stupid, however, so it shouldn't come to that.

The only hiccup, as it were, in my otherwise smooth plans to return the proper measure of power to Mer, was the dratted Prince Marley. He and the nomad girl Katjia followed us. I knew it was foolish of us to leave in the dead of night, but Uncle was insistent, and we paid a price for it. The two of them might be sworn to secrecy, but they are not stupid at all, and I fear that I shall rue the day I didn't have them killed in the forest. However, all of my complex schemes will collapse around my ears if I kill the prince now. We can't afford to have Laitmea go to war with us on her own terms.

So for now I will let King Zavaxer work out a hostage return on his own. Hopefully, Marley doesn't do anything too detrimental to the plan before Redgenold stages his coup. I will need to return ahead of the rest of the Third Order in order to steal the necessary documents beforehand, and I can't do that if his royal highness is causing problems.

So far, he and Katjia haven't really done anything, but I suppose that it's only a matter of time. Carsten has been watching them carefully, and he has nothing to report. But he will also be needed for the false coup, and for instating my informant's candidate after the Queen's private documents become public. I will need to think up a solution to the Marley problem before then. One that doesn't involve returning his mangled corpse to his family.

Veena

* * *

Kanara

It had been five days since Katjia disappeared. Every time Kanara thought about it for too long, he felt sick.

He knew that he needed to stay with the rest of his family. He couldn't leave them leaderless to search the countryside for his sister, however much he might want to. Katjia must have had a very good reason for running away with the prince, and, wherever she had gone, she was an adept fighter and could take care of herself. That didn't make it hurt any less.

He knew that if he stayed in the same spot, she would be able to find him when she returned, but every time he thought of it, his mind tried to say *if she returned.*

Worst of all, she hadn't thought to wake him and say that she was going. If there had been such a good reason for it, he wouldn't have stopped her, which meant that she had either deliberately done something foolish, or she didn't care if she hurt him. Neither explanation sat well.

He had been able to purchase enough food for a month, extra saddle grade leather, and repairs to many of their damaged possessions, all with the sale of only one horse. The royal family had granted permission for the tribe to stay indefinitely while they searched for the missing prince. But none of it mattered, not without his little sister.

Kanara had taken to pacing in the courtyard, while the rest of his family explored the wonders of the city or conversed with the other princes and princesses. If things had been different, he might have loved the opportunity to see the sights of Laitmea, taste the country's food, and converse with its people. As it was, he preferred to delegate these tasks to his cousins and wander their camp alone.

He turned around for what might have been the tenth, or possibly the ten thousandth time, and saw a horse cantering up the path towards the gate. Dashing forward, he flung the gates open to admit the beast, his heart thudding. It was Petrushka, Katjia's horse. She was breathing heavily, eyes rolling, legs studded with burrs. Kanara felt as if his stomach was sinking into his boots. The saddle was empty.

* * *

Jessimin

Jessimin absently fingered the fine cream-colored lace on her skirt. It was a beautiful skirt, really, the pale golden color of new butter, with tier after tier of ruffles, each fringed with the slimmest band of lace roses. Beautiful, but not at all practical for sneaking about in the dank lower basement to turn off the furnace.

After some consideration, Jessimin began to unlace the dress. It was difficult to manage without a maid to help, but eventually the shell of the dress fell to a heap on the floor, and she stepped out. She removed her top two petticoats as well, and glanced at her reflection in her room's full-length mirror.

Without the leg-of-mutton sleeves she had begged the tailor for, her arms were like two pale sticks poking out of her shift. There was also the issue of her undergarments being quite low cut. It wasn't as if she had much to show, but her corset made certain that anything that could be displayed *was*. If anyone saw her like this… but no, that was the point. Without her bulky skirts in the way, she could move stealthily and make her way in the basement without being caught. Still feeling frighteningly naked, Jessimin slipped out of her room and down the hall to the staircase.

Her stocking feet made muffled thumps, raising small puffs of coal dust as she traveled lower into the bowels of the palace. She felt even more jumpy leaving the staircase behind, for despite having lived in the palace for her entire life, Jessimin had never ventured into the lower basement. It wasn't

92

just a matter of propriety. The basement was *creepy*. Curiosity had led her down to the bottom step before, but she had always thought it best to leave the dark and coal smeared recesses to those *paid* to be there.

Of course, she knew the layout of the lower basement, from servants' chatter and her father's extensive remodeling plans, but her confidence in her abilities to find and turn down the furnace had been largely affected. She was sure that she *could* do it, but whether she could do it in a safe and timely manner was another question altogether. But Pippy and Mayzin had put their trust in her, and she knew she could not disappoint. She made her way forward in the semidarkness, one hand trailing along the grimy wall.

In theory, the furnace would be one room away, and a simple left turn down the second passage she came to should bring it into view. In practice, even these simple directions were hard to follow, with her heart pounding and her arms trembling as they were. She turned, and much to her relief, heard the dull roar that could only be the furnace.

It was an impregnable black monster, squatting in the dark. It took up almost the entire room with its metal bulk and flaming maw. Heat washed over Jessimin, and she immediately began to sweat despite her state of undress. Feeling much like a minuscule knight about to do battle with a fully grown dragon, she surveyed the multitudinous nobs and levers dimly lit by the coal fire glow. *Nothing was labeled!*

Fighting down a deranged laugh, she circled around to the side, ducking under pipes undoubtedly carrying hotter than hot water to various parts of the palace. If she shut off one of these by accident... No one would miss the furnace for one day in the hottest week of spring, but the instant the newfangled plumbing system went down, the servants would be launching an investigation and all hope of rescuing letters from the furnace would be lost.

Then, on the far side, she spotted it. A gear so massive that it couldn't possibly be for one pipe. She turned it clockwise, and it spun with ease. The furnace roared, playing the part of dragon very well, and the room became even hotter. Feeling slightly hysterical, and also like she might faint, she grasped the wheel again and turned it the other way. It was much harder.

After a moment, the gear began to burn her hands, so she hastily let go. She gathered the skirt of her shift over her hands and turned again, heaving harder and harder, until she couldn't move it another inch. Ducking back out under the pipes, she saw that the fire had come down from its roaring high to smolder insolently in the gloom. As she watched, several more coals winked out. Satisfied that her dragon was vanquished, Jessimin trotted out of the basement, and once she was clear of the stairs, broke into a run.

Safely ensconced in her room, she turned her attention to getting her dress back on, trying not to think of how she would need to go back tomorrow. It turned out to be difficult enough to dress without a maid that by the time she was clothed again, the basement was a distant memory.

* * *

Dinner that evening was a small affair, with the elder royalty holding a formal meeting. Addmaleta presided over a small feast of roast pheasant and a light fish soup. The was an obligatory salad course, veal floating in an unidentifiable orange sauce, and for dessert, a delicate crepe-like pastry that Jessimin was sure she should probably know the name of.

Nikolous was away at the meeting and Alloysius was sullen for not having been invited, though it was only recently that he had been allowed to dine with family instead of in the nursery. Xeno was visiting one of his many Lady loves, and Kestly simply wasn't there. Redge pled a debilitating illness, whose symptoms were mainly fabricated, and so they numbered five.

At Redge's declaration of absence, Jessimin caught a dark look from Pippy, but it would have been both rude and unproductive to skip out of a meal. Their plan was in place. Though Jessimin had not wanted to dwell on the dormant furnace before, thoughts of it now seemed comforting. Soon they would have more information. Soon, they would not be sitting idly by, waiting for Redge's nefarious plans to come to fruition.

* * *

As she was being undressed by Loretta that night, Jessimin's mind was far away, speculations about her older brother running wild. She was brought back to Eretz with a bump when Loretta suddenly exclaimed, "My word, your underthings! Whatever could have happened?" It was only then that Jessimin remembered that she had been wearing a lovely clean shift this morning. Now, it was smudged with coal and cobwebs. To her horror, she could also see that the red hot wheel had burned several small holes through the material. Silently berating herself, and hoping that she hadn't jeopardized the entire plan, Jessimin mumble something that could have been "oh, nothing," or perhaps "exploring."

"Well not much we can do about it now," Loretta huffed, with an all too knowing look. "What do you want me to do about it?"

"Just get rid of it... only make sure no one knows! Daddy would be furious, with the rate I go through dresses. He says I'll clean out the whole treasury for frilly things." She bit her lip, hoping that if she appeared distraught enough, Loretta wouldn't push to know exactly *how* she had ruined the garment. It worked.

"Well, fine thing like this, I can patch up the holes and give it to my daughter. She'll be big enough for it soon."

Loretta folded the offending article with a satisfied snort and took it with her once Jessimin was settled in her night things. There were undeniable perks to being a princess.

* * *

Veena

Carsten says that his two prisoners are proving quite contrary. The girl, Katjia, has a mouth more foul than a seasoned sailor and enjoys cursing her captors. She plumbs the depths of her vocabulary, working out new insults to hurl at him every time he opens the door.

All in all, I'm quite impressed. I even learned a few new words myself. I don't quite know what to make of her, otherwise. She's pretty enough, but wearing some ridiculous smelly horse leather tunic and skirt. It's sturdy enough to be a sort of armor, I guess, but wholly unflattering.

She's a tough fighter and gave two of Carsten's men goose-egg-sized lumps on their heads before they subdued her. If circumstances were different, I would take her as an apprentice, but as it is, I'm wary of anyone so willing to go riding halfway across the country with a total stranger simply on principle. She says that she did it because Marley helped her, and she wanted to help him. There was no way he could have tracked us so far without a horse.

But that still doesn't explain why she didn't just lend him her steed. Of all the people in Eretz, why is she the one to become tangled up in our plot? She can tell us that it was chance, but personally, I think it has more to do with her willingness to help others and her strength of character. I fear that she may prove to be a truly dangerous enemy, but I daren't have her killed.

Marley is a little easier to grasp. He followed us because he feared what we might do to his family, nothing more. He is more easily frightened than

Katjia and therefore easier to control. Still, he isn't stupid, and he has pitted himself against me fully. He is only safe because he is being kept in a locked room under guard. He doesn't insult Carsten, but instead badgers him with endless questions about the construction of pirates' ships.

At first we feared that he was somehow hoping to plan an escape or gather intelligence with which to furnish the Laitmeans, but when we went through the meager store of belongings in his satchel, we found that he has made a habit of drawing ships. His obsession is a little disconcerting, particularly because it is undiminished by the fact that he is being held hostage. He wants to know everything there is to know about ships. He asks questions that only a professional shipwright could know and expects Carsten to find him the answers.

I know that Carsten despises both of them, but I don't trust anyone else. He sits by the door, growing ever more sour. I've told him that it is only temporary, but it doesn't do any good.

Of course, we won't let Zavaxer go through with his hostage negotiations. Because I've already taken over all of my Uncle's positions, it's easy enough for me to ensure that none of his letters reach Lyrah. Let the royal family and their pet tribe worry about their missing members. It might make them more suspicious towards Mer, but that doesn't matter. Having to return the pair to Laitmea would only complicate things now.

I've talked with Carsten about the problems they're causing, but he doesn't have any good ideas right now, despite having so much time to sit and think about it. Yesterday, he said that he'll tell me if he comes up with a solution, and I need to stop bothering him. I don't know if I will stop, though. Bothering him is a sure way of getting a kiss.

* * *

Mayzin

Katjia's horse has returned without her. What this means for her and Marley, I don't know, but I fear that if Redge is behind their disappearance, we must act quickly. If the furnace doesn't hold the secrets, I don't know what we'll do.

Father has sent out more scouts to look for them, but so far they've found nothing. From what the other nomads say, if Katjia didn't want to be followed, she won't have left any discernible trail. Everyone is on edge.

Cousin Addmaleta is still searching for her missing bracelet, along with a few other small trinkets that have also vanished. Next to a missing brother, missing jewels seem like a small matter, but if the incidents are somehow connected, we might have more luck finding answers.

Pippy thinks they are not related, as if nobody who steals bracelets would be interesting in kidnapping a prince too.

* * *

Pippy took a peek at my diary and said that, just to clarify, she thinks that the mysterious vanishings are unrelated because the jewelry went missing after Marley did. Maybe she's right. She definitely has no manners. Just because I trust her more than Redge and leave this out when she's around doesn't mean that she has a right to read what's in it.

98

I'm only glad that she didn't flip back far enough to see all the letters from Bella. Pippy doesn't know how to keep her mouth shut, and there's a bit of gossip I wouldn't want to get out. I had a hard enough time convincing Bella's mother that I wasn't responsible for her daughter's elopement. I don't need my work undermined by my sister's loose lips.

* * *

Jessimin

The following morning, any comfort in the thought of retrieving letters from the furnace was gone, replaced by the certain dread of having to do battle with the black beast *again*.

"Can we do the old orange dress today, Loretta? I'm not doing much, and I can change for dinner."

"Not wanting to ruin another pretty new thing?" the maid quipped, but she got her way. The orange dress would be by far the easiest to undo later, as it laced up the front. Jessimin made a mental note to ask her tailor for more such dresses in the future, perhaps with lace and leg-of-mutton sleeves. It was the height of fashion, after all.

Loretta was just attempting to rein in Jessimin's wild mass of curls when Pippy entered her room by the side door and flounced onto her bed. She was the only child in the family not to have inherited their parents' flaxen hair, and Jessimin had ever been jealous of her long, straight, tomato red locks, today wound into an effortless swirl of braids.

Envy seemed to be the mood of the day, for Pippy greeted her with a sigh and said, "Oh, I wish I could wear orange or russet or whatever that color is. It's ravishing on you, but I'd look every bit a furnace in it."

A knowing look flashed between the sisters, and Jessimin said, "I think I can manage from here. Would you mind leaving us, Loretta?" The maid left, with on eyebrow raised, for it was quite clear that *no one* could manage Jessimin's

100

hair.

Shortly after Loretta had departed, Mayzin entered and set about finishing the haphazard bun Loretta had started.

"Personally," Mayzin began, "I'm all for checking the furnace now and getting it over with. All this delay just makes me nervous that some nincompoop will decide they want the heat on in this weather. If someone turns the furnace on, the letters go up in flames, and goodness knows they'd be keeping a closer eye on things after that."

Jessimin handed her a hairpin and added, "And goodness knows I'd like to go to the basement right now and finish this job. And never ever set foot there again for as long as I live, if it comes to it."

Pippy arranged her cerulean skirts about her and sighed. "You're right, you're both right, but it's precisely *because* we've only got one shot at this that we have to wait. We need to be absolutely certain that Redge, or anyone, for that matter, will have had time to try and burn any letters we might want to read. Any post delivered to the palace last night will be handed out *now*. He won't have even read his letters, let alone burned them. After tea will be good enough."

"I don't think I shall be able to stand the wait," Mayzin moaned, echoing Jessimin's thoughts.

* * *

The second trip to the basement was no less harrowing than the first. Jessimin supposed that she was a tad too old to be afraid of the dark, but she doubted that anyone could be old enough not to fear dueling a furnace in their undergarments.

She had almost wanted to pawn the job off on one of her sisters, but the thought of how Mayzin or Pippy might handle themselves down beneath the palace had quelled the thought almost instantly. One cobweb and every window on the first floor could shatter from the screaming.

The furnace was not a dragon today. It was still menacing, but without its fire, it seemed much smaller. More like a poisonous snake or a mad dog.

There were still a few patches of glowing coals in the depths of its maw, but they were not her concern.

Beneath the many chutes and pipes that emptied into the furnaces' heart, a heap of papers lay. There were lots. Many more than Jessimin had anticipated, and she had no way of knowing which belonged to Redge. She hadn't any time to waste, either. Servants would be down to tend to business sooner or later. Realizing that she needed to take *all* the letters with her, she hurriedly reached into the still uncomfortably hot vent and began to stuff handfuls of letters into her pockets. When they were full, and her hands smudged with coal dust, there were still more letters.

With no other options, she stuffed them down the front of her corset. When she was sure that she had extracted every scrap of correspondence, she hurried around to the back, almost clocking her own head on a pipe, and yanked the wheel around clockwise. The dragon roared to life once more, and she bolted out of the room. She was almost to the stairway when she froze.

Feet clattering down the steps!

Servants were coming, lugging coal to feed the insatiable monster. Jessimin pressed herself into the far corner of the room, hoping that she had accumulated enough filth to hid the white of her shift. Letters scraped against her collar bones as she trembled. Fragments of conversation drifted down to her as a pair of men came into view.

"...and check that everything's adjusted properly, the water's not been getting hot enough."

"Ruddy complicated system. It's always falling apart."

To her relief, the men were fully occupied with their bags of coal and didn't notice her. Soon after they had rounded the corner, however, a shout rang out down the hall.

"Now how the hell are we supposed to fit all this lot in here? It hasn't even burned through half of what we put in yesterday!"

"They must have gotten the amounts mixed up. We can't be meant to fill it so high, " the second man said.

"Lets go find some higher up who knows what this behemoth needs."

The two sprinted back through the room and up the stairs, once again ignoring Jessimin.

She waited until her heart had stopped pounding, then decided that it would be best to move now, before the servants came back with reinforcements. She hurried up the stairs, so wrapped up in panic that she almost collided with the figure coming down.

"Princess Jessimin! What is the meaning of this?" Her stomach gave a horrible lurch. Bernard, the head of staff. The butler was pointedly looking slightly above her left shoulder, so as not to see her near nakedness, but it was too much to hope that he had missed the proliferation of papers sticking up from her bust. It was difficult to say in that moment who was more embarrassed.

Jessimin spluttered incoherently for a moment, trying to think of some remotely plausible reason for her to be undressed and in the basement with her corset full of other people's correspondence.

Even the truth sounded too far fetched in her mind. She wondered what would happen if she did try to explain herself, as all alibis became exponentially more ridiculous when spoken aloud.

After a pregnant pause, Bernard declared, "You know, I really don't even want to know. Lets just pretend that this never happened and go on with our lives."

"That's fine by me," Jessimin whispered, going more than a little weak at the knees from relief. They both hesitated a moment longer, then rushed in opposite directions as quickly as possible.

Jessimin slammed the door to her room and leaned against it, letting out a moan. She was never *ever* going into the basement again, clothes or no. And she might just die of embarrassment if she ever had to look Bernard in the eye again. Her only comfort, small as it was, was that he would not tell anyone what had happened, if only to preserve his dignity.

* * *

BERNARD
AND
JESSIMIN

Katjia

Katjia wanted to scream from frustration. Less than a week ago, she had been bringing her family safely into a new land, her brother at her side. Now she was imprisoned by pirates, sharing a cell with a Laitmean prince. She had lost her horse, her staff, and her dignity in the fight in the woods. The rest of her belongings had been seized upon their arrival in Pirate's Cove. Only the clothes on her back were left to remind her who she was and what she stood for.

She didn't for one moment regret her decision to help Marley. It was clear that the pirate Veena was embroiled in some dastardly plot that would put not only Marley's family, but hers, in peril. It was, in a way, a blessing that she was here, even if she knew that her brother would be worried sick about her.

There might not be any way to let him know that she was safe or that he should prepare for the worst sort of the betrayal from the pirates, but she was close enough to the source of her misery to have some hope of influencing whatever plots swirled around her. If she could free herself, or talk her way into a better position, she could protect every resident of the palace from afar. No, helping Marley had been the right decision, and she didn't hold their imprisonment against him at all. What she did hold against him was his attitude now that they were locked up.

While she spent every waking moment trying think up a way out of their predicament, Marley was still acting as if they had never left Lyrah's

105

dockyards. Every time Carsten poked his head into the room where they were being kept, Marley wanted to debate the best type of sails for stormy conditions or ask hundreds of inane questions about the pirates' shipbuilding techniques. When their jailer was absent, he spent the long hours doodling ships in his diary or bemoaning the fact that he was so close to the pirates' well-renowned vessels, yet unable to set foot on even one of them.

Katjia knew that this must be his way of coping with their situation. As awful as their imprisonment was for her, she had spent the formative years of her life in far worse conditions. The prince must have been suffering all the more, given his pampered upbringing. Still, it was annoying beyond words to be stuck in a confined space with a boy who only wanted to talk about ships.

There were brief moments when she could see just how terrified the prince really was, especially each time the door opened. He would always flinch each time their jailer came and went, and Katjia sometimes felt that these moments were the only things keeping her from strangling Marley with her bare hands. Still, as much as she hated to admit it, she knew that if he were not there, imprisonment might very well have broken her long ago. There was something comforting about having a cell-mate, even one as odd as Marley.

She tried a few times to bring up the idea of escape, but even if the prince had been willing to discuss it, she feared who might listen in. As the days crept by, she felt herself becoming as tense as a coiled spring. She gave up trying to talk to anyone, except to ask Carsten again and again if there was any hope of them being released. Even though his answer remained the same, the ritual of asking him helped her to keep her sanity. Just as she was sure that Marley's ritual of talking about ships for a few hours before retreating to the corner of the room to rock himself to sleep allowed him to keep his. She wondered, for how long could they keep their rituals up?

* * *

Marley

I don't think that Veena is really a loyal pirate. The King has been debating how to best negotiate releasing us hostages to Laitmea and fretting about how much ransom is too much. I'm certain that the wants some kind of peaceful agreement with my family. I don't like the thought of costing Aunty Trill so much gold, but given the circumstances, it does seem like the best possible outcome. But from everything I heard, the diplomat King Zavaxer sent to complain was not nearly so peaceable.

I know that Veena tattled on him being a traitor, but when she's on her own, she seems just as bloodthirsty as he was. Perhaps they're both traitors, and they had some kind of squabble?

Anyway, Veena might pretend to support the kings' hostage return plan when there's pirates of the king's council around, but I could have sworn that she and Carsten were plotting how best to dispose of Katjia and myself this morning. They seem to *want* a war with Laitmea, and killing me wouldn't be a half-bad way of starting one. Katjia might make me nervous, but Veena makes me *terrified*.

* * *

Jessimin

Mayzin and Pippy slipped through Jessimin's door almost before she was fully dressed again. As she tied the last bow on the orange dress, they were already sorting through the heap of letters on the floor.

"We'll only look for letters addressed to our brother," Mayzin stated, tossing aside a crumpled card. "No use being nosy. If it hasn't got his name on it, toss it."

"Oh, please!" Pippy snorted, "We've gone to all this trouble anyway, what's the harm in reading mother's post. Or father's, or anyone's, for that matter?"

"Because it isn't right! We've got reason to believe that Redge is planning something really terrible, otherwise I wouldn't have agreed to this at all." Mayzin continued to throw letters aside after barely glancing at them.

Pippy rolled her eyes and began to read. "There are bound to be some salacious tidbits in here, you know."

"And we're no closer to finding out what Redge is up to, while you waste time." Jessimin added, knowing full well that if time had permitted, she would be on Pippy's side. A chance to read the gossip of the entire palace was not something you came by every day.

"Here's one," she said, spotting Redge's name in the pile.

"Dear Master Redgenold," she read aloud, "Please be advised that the pigeon mail service is only to be used for messages of utmost urgency and importance. It is not for sending twelve letters a day. Yours sincerely, Garth Peggerston,

Post Master General."

"Oh, no," said Pippy, dropping the note she was holding with a moan, "That wasn't Redge, it was me. I wanted to write to Duke Javis' son without anyone getting suspicious, so I signed Redge's name." She turned a shade of scarlet that almost matched her hair as she spoke.

"And the Duke's son responded, I take it?" Mayzin asked.

"*Twelve letters a day?*" Jessimin added with a wicked grin.

"It wasn't anything untoward," Pippy said matter-of-factually, returning to scouring the remaining letters. "We only agreed that we are quite interested in getting to know each other better. We've barely spoken since we met at the welcome ball for Mer's diplomat. It was mostly introductory. We weren't professing our undying love or anything interesting. I would never be so stupid as to put that in a letter, even if we were at that point already."

"Best to find the postmaster general and apologize, then," Mayzin said, letting the subject drop. There was still a glint in her eye that let Jessimin know they would be teasing their sister about Duke Javis' son at a later date.

"Here! Jessimin exclaimed, "This one is actually Redge's... and oh, dear. It's not really what I was hoping for..." she began to read aloud, with an expression of growing horror.

"Dear Master Redgenold, son of Redgenold. On your last letter: Yes, it is undeniable that you are in the line of succession. Extensive documentation can be found to validate your extant title of prince. Per your agreement with the *Third Order* via yours truly, upon the deaths of the elder royals, this documentation will be made public.

"However, our continued support of your planned coup is contingent on your ability to honor your end of the bargain. With only a thousand men at arms able to mobilize, we cannot risk outright war. It is imperative that you maintain utmost secrecy until you are prepared to strike. Burn this letter, Vee."

"That's horrible!" Mayzin shrieked, as soon as Jessimin reached the end of the letter. "He's going to have us all killed by some mysterious order so he can be king?"

"He must be crazy," Jessimin agreed, knowing that her face had gone stark white. "He must be absolutely insane. I'd have never thought my own big brother would…"

"It's despicable!" Mayzin clutched at her skirts. "Absolutely despicable! Pippy, forget we made fun of you for writing Duke Javis' son. We need to find a way of stopping Redge! …Pippy?"

Their older sister wasn't paying attention, though. Pippy was reading a different letter, eyes wide, one hand over her mouth.

"Pippy?" Jessimin asked tentatively. Pippy let out a guffaw. She fell back on the rug, laughing and clutching the letter, tears streaming down her face. Mayzin made a grab for it, but Pippy rolled away, still crying with laughter.

"Pippy, what's so funny?"

"Our brother is plotting a coup! This is no time for games, Quipeneay!"

Pippy kicked her feet up on the end of Jessimin's bedstead, and lying flat on her back began to read the letter between gasps and giggles.

"To my dearest Kestly," she began, "I know that our relationship has been purely mercenary, but since our last meeting, I have been able to think of nothing but the softness of your milk-white skin!"

Mayzin gave a snort and fell back onto Jessimin's bed.

Pippy continued, "your cherry red lips are like an intoxicating brew, the slimness of your waist a fine wine. I feel, even now, that your eyes still stare into mine, and I would be lost in their cerulean depths, tangled in your flaxen hair!"

Jessimin was laughing to the point of wheezing now, almost unable to hear Pippy as she took up the letter again.

"Kestly, Kestly! I have fallen quite in love! Your presence is all my soul desires. Come back, kiss me again, and I shall be the happiest of all men!"

"Again?" Mayzin exclaimed, "She's been kissing some man?"

"Shush, I haven't even come to the best part!" Pippy laughed, "Kestly, my darling, my star, my beautiful princess! I care not if you have aught to sell me, lo, even if you were the poorest beggar in the land, I would have you still. I adore the very ground you tread on, I shall kiss your feet! Say we shall meet again, business or no! (Yet let it be noted that if trinkets you have, the Tuesday after next would be ideal for a meeting. My coffers are growing empty.) Ah,

Kestly my love, write back swiftly! I shall not breathe easy until I know if you are mine, oh angel. With most ardent love, Tobias."

"She's kissing some man named Tobias?" Jessimin exclaimed, throwing Redge's letter of treason aside, "Let Redge kill us all tomorrow, my life is complete!"

* * *

READING
        MAIL

Veena

King Zavaxer has learned that Laitmea's King and Queen are unaware that we have Marley and Katjia, much less that we wish to return them. To be fair, only the First Order is particularly interested in getting them off our hands. Still, Zavaxer was supposed to be kept in the dark. Unfortunately, one of his advisors noticed me disposing of a letter that I was supposed to have delivered to the capital.

I pled ignorance, and claimed that it was not his letter, but a piece of my own mail that I burned. In a way it was true, seeing as I've been heavily reworking every piece of Zavaxer's post that I do send on.

I'm not sure that he believes me, however. It is unreasonable to think that Laitmea wouldn't want Marley back immediately. Had the King's letters been sent, we would already be halfway done negotiating his release to them. But the Third Order needed more time to prepare, while I was busy manipulating Redgenold. Now, everything is in place.

The mad prince thinks that he is leading a coup against his family, complete with assassins and the men of the Third Order. In reality, the assassinations are doomed to failure, given the number and competency of the palace guards. They will, however, sow chaos and divert everyone's attention.

Carsten and I will return to Laitmea, where I will prepare to steal the documents necessary to bring down the monarchy, and Carsten will lead a short and futile charge against the palace for the sole purpose of causing a distraction and discrediting Redgenold.

This rebellion will be quelled by the waiting troops of my informant's suitable candidate, and he shall subsequently be crowned King. His first act will be to change the accord with Mer to allow us pirates free reign. Carsten and I will then return, heroes, to Pirates Cove. In the face of our victory, Zavaxer will be forced out of the order.

Everything is ready now, so it is not really such a problem that Zavaxer knows that his letters aren't making it to Laitmea, I hope. I will still need to talk things through with Carsten, however. If Marley is returned to his family now, it could ruin everything we have worked for.

* * *

Mayzin

I still don't know what has become of Marley, and the worry has been sitting in my stomach like a cannonball. But now we know for sure that Redge is planning a treasonous betrayal of our whole family.

His letters, stolen by my favorite sister, Jessimin, were full of his plans to kill us all and take over the government by force. He's going to make himself king, if he can. I only hope that Marley is all right.

I spent a few hours talking it over with Jessi and Pippy, and we have arrived at a reasonable plan for dealing with our insane brother. (Not to be confused with our other brothers, who are only slightly less crazed, but markedly more well mannered.)

We cannot bring the letters to our parents for two reasons: Redge doesn't know that we know, and we would like to keep it that way until we can be sure that he will suffer reasonable consequences for his actions. Telling anyone now would just give him a chance to bolt and join the mysterious *Third Order* he's going to use to attack us.

Also, if anyone (yes, you Pippy) reads my first few entries, they will know that the so-called adults in our family are not the most practical of people. They would spring into action at the mere mention of treason, but whether that action would be good....

We don't need Aunty Trill feeding our brother to Dart, especially not before he's been questioned. We need to know who his contact is and what else she might be plotting.

Personally, I think the person writing to him is Mer's diplomat's niece, Violet. The letters were signed V, which fits, and given the conversation Jessi overheard, it seems pretty clear that she was pushing him to become king. This means that she, and likely her uncle as well, aren't followers of the pirate law. They're part of the Third Order, whatever that is. It does change things a bit, and throws their meeting with Aunty Trill and Uncle Dowlin into a new light. Who knows if the pirates actually want different Laitmean leadership? Who knows why they were asking for free reign to attack our sea trade?

Anyway, we needed a plan for how to deal with Redge that doesn't involve telling Aunty Trill, Uncle Dowlin, mother, or father. Suddenly, we remembered Aunty Ettalara and Uncle Dowlin. The most sane members of the royal family, probably. At least they're far enough away from the capital that they couldn't tell Redge that we know, or attack him, or anything. Then Pippy had a brilliant idea: She'll tell mother that she wants to have her coming out to society at their estate, rather than the palace.

Mother will, of course, jump at the chance to send the three of us away to plan the party. She hates debutante balls almost as much as she hates traitors, and Aunty Ettalara loves them, so it's only natural. It's a few months to Pippy's birthday, but it's only natural to get a head start. And this way, Redge has no reason to suspect anything. We can be safely across the country, planning his demise, and no one need be the wiser.

* * *

If anyone (Pippy) has noticed a problem with our plan, never fear. I needed to take a break from writing to eat something. Regular meals have become a rarity around here with Marley missing and everyone running about trying to figure out where he's gone and what the pirates want and what's the matter with Mer and who keeps stealing things.

So, now. How are we going to ensure that Redge doesn't try anything while we're days away, figuring out how to stop him? We need someone trustworthy to follow him like a shadow and report anything suspicious. Seeing as Pippy and Jessi are the only other trustworthy people around, I thought we were stuck, but then we came across a certain piece of Kestly's mail. Our big sister has some big secrets. And we will be using those secrets to blackmail her. She'll not be telling anyone anything, if she doesn't want the world to know about the boy she's been seeing.

Redge can plot all he likes, I think we've done him one better.

* * *

Katjia

Marley was gone when Katjia woke. As tired of his antics as she had become, she still found solitude disconcerting. Her first thought was that she was tending to the horses in the dead of night, but as she rubbed the sleep from her eyes, she could see that she was still in her cell.

Bleary-eyed, she tried to make sense of what was going on. The last thing she remembered from the prior evening was Carsten leaving abruptly. She had eaten the meal they were provided with, but not really tasted it, and she had soon slipped back into the depressive funk of her own thoughts, drifting off to sleep while Marley babbled on about something. As much as she pretended to hate it, his voice was a comfort.

Her earlier thoughts of escape had been all but muted by the sheer boredom she had experienced over the past several days. Now however, she felt some of her old self returning. She briefly wondered if the prince had found some way to escape, but she discounted the thought. If he had, he would not have abandoned her. It was far more probable that Veena had had him removed sometime in the night. She could have decided that solitary confinement would simply be better for them, but more likely some kind of hostage exchange had been worked out. Perhaps the prince was already on his way back to his family, in which case she was sure that he would try to have her rescued soon. It was more likely, however, that the pirates would want to return only his dead body.

Their King might have presented himself as peaceful, but Carsten and Veena were certainly not, and Katjia doubted that the prospect of war would dissuade them from drowning Marley as soon as ransom was collected. She shuddered at the thought. However much sharing a cell with him had irked her, he was still the boy who had offered her family sanctuary, and a sweet boy at that. What was more, if the pirates were no longer protecting him, she was now in danger too. Whatever the case, her fortunes were not about to improve. She thought of her brother and almost cried. She should have spent every waking moment trying to think of a way to get back to her family. She had allowed herself to become despondent and had failed them all.

As if to confirm all of her fears, the door was yanked open a moment later, and Carsten stormed in to grab her. Katjia wasn't quite sure how long she had been locked up for, but it was still a surreal experience to be outside now. She felt like a ghost in her own body as the pirate dragged her down the street. There was a faint glow of dawn on the eastern horizon, but no one else seemed to be awake in the pirates' makeshift town.

She hoped that whatever Carsten had in store for her would be over quickly. She had already caused her family enough suffering, she didn't want to have to endure a grisly end herself. She hoped that Carsten wouldn't be the last person whom she saw. He was a good enough looking man, with tanned skin and long dark hair, and he hadn't been unnecessarily cruel, but his unwavering devotion to Veena and their plots made him a thoroughly despicable creature.

Any girl who would arrange the death of her uncle like that and take prisoners with so little thought was not worth an ounce of any man's love. She wondered if Veena would have cared for him if he hadn't been so easy to manipulate.

Carsten brought her to the massive pirate ship at the cove's dock. Katjia was surprised to see the vessel floating in so little water. She vaguely remembered Marley telling her that this was possible; it hadn't seemed important at the time.

As she went up the rickety plank into the ship, she wondered if there would be any dock at all when she disembarked.

Much to her surprise, Veena was waiting for her at the rear of the ship.

More surprising still, was a fact that she was holding Marley, with a knife to his throat. Katjia wondered how she had managed to sleep through his being dragged out of their shared accommodations.

There were a few other pirates on board, to man the oars, most of them familiar from the night of the ambassador's assassination. Veena smiled at her, and said "how sweet of you to join us. I was just telling Marley here that my plans to overthrow Laitmean government and allow us pirates access to all of their ships are moving apace. King Zavaxer and his peaceful protestations will soon be deposed, and a new golden age for Mer will begin."

"I didn't know those were your plans," said Katjia.

"Well, my real plans are a fair bit more complicated than that, but I can't have the two of you getting in the way, so you've already heard everything I'm going to tell you about them."

"So King Zavaxer isn't going to have a chance to give us back to Laitmea for ransom then, is he?"

"No, what an astute observation. Carsten and I will be leaving the pirates shortly to assist in the next stage of my plans. We won't be here to keep tabs on you, and unfortunately you know far too much for us to leave you at the mercy of King Zavaxer. We can't kill you, though without arousing his suspicions, so it will be best for all concerned if the two of you appear to have escaped. Carsten and I will, of course, volunteer to search for you, giving us a chance to go back to Laitmea without anyone knowing. For once, you actually turned out to be useful."

Katjia wasn't quite sure what to make of this speech, but she *was* sure that she and Marley weren't actually going to escape. She hoped that they weren't actually going to be killed either. Not even Marley had the audacity to ask, though.

* * *

Jessimin

Jessimin knocked on the door to her sister Kestly's room, holding her breath. Hopefully, she would open the door, but Kessie had an annoying habit of sneaking out of windows. Remembering the diplomat's ball, Jessimin wondered if her third-oldest sibling was already making a run for it. Pippy and Mayzin stood directly behind her, looking just as nervous as she felt.

Blackmailing their sister was not something that came easily to them, even if it was justified. Redge needed to stay in the dark about how much they knew until they had a good way of stopping him. Pippy had been keeping the letters they had filched from the furnace in her pocket. Those that hadn't been relevant were already burning up as originally intended.

After settling on a course of action, the three had spent the afternoon making arrangements with their mother to leave for Aunt Ettalara's. They would depart early the next morning, taking a boat down the river to the port at Firdell, and then a carriage to her estate. Now, the sun was long set, and they were setting the last piece in motion.

They breathed a collective sigh of relief when Kestly opened her door. She wasn't wearing a night dress, nor did she look like she had been asleep, as she should have been at that hour. She was wearing a blue party dress and a traveling cloak, and had her hair braided and set with sapphires. Her window was ajar, as if she had just returned through it. She smelled faintly of smoke and cheap liquor, as if she had spent the evening in a lower city tavern. She probably had.

"What are you three doing here at this ungodly hour?" she asked, "some of us are trying to sleep!"

Pippy took a good look at Kestly, and raised one eyebrow. "Some people in this palace *are* trying to sleep, no doubt, but you must think we're halfwits to say that you are one of them. I'm not even going to ask where you've been."

"I'm of age, I can make my own decisions," Kestly said defensively, closing the door slightly.

"We're not here to debate that," said Mayzin, stepping on Pippy's foot with a look that said *Be careful. We can't have her running away on us.* "We're here about a certain letter you wrote, and you'd best not close this door on us, or who knows who might hear about it."

Kestly tossed her head back, thinking for a minute, then sighed. "Very well, come in. I know when I'm being blackmailed."

Kestly's room was lit by a smattering of candles, which cast just enough light to show the disheveled state of its occupant. She closed her window and drew the curtains, then sat down at the most disorganized vanity Jessimin had ever seen.

"Don't mind if I do my hair while you talk. It's been a long evening."

"You mean a long morning," said Mayzin, nodding at the clock.

Kestly shrugged, and pulled one of the sapphire pins out of her hair, discarding it on a small tray. "So you were the ones sneaking letters out of the furnace. Suspicious of me?"

"Hardly," snorted Jessimin. "We're all well aware of your lawless ways. Fancy yourself Mother's miniature, don't you? I saw you slipping out of the window at the ball. I could have followed if I wanted to. No, it's Redge we were interested in."

"Then what are you doing here? I haven't mentioned him in any of my letters. Frankly, I don't remember any letter containing something bad enough for you to worry yourselves about. I'm not foolish enough to trust all of my secrets to the furnace, and rightly so, it seems."

Mayzin looked concerned at that. "You're saying you have worse than Tobias?"

To their shock, Kestly rocked back in her chair and laughed.

"Him?" She caught their expressions and righted herself, wiping her eyes on the backs of her hands. "Oh, he thinks we're something of an item."

"You're not?" said Pippy, surprised.

"I sell him odd trinkets I find lying around. It's a purely mercenary relationship. How else can I fund my life of excess? Father made it clear that I wasn't getting any more pocket money since I came of age, even if I haven't wed. Tobias knows he's not the only boy, he just likes to kid himself. Not even that good looking, really."

"You stole Addmaleta's bracelet, didn't you!" Mayzin exclaimed.

"I can't believe she noticed it was gone. I've taken half a dozen things from her room and she's never missed one before."

"Noticed it was gone? She's been almost as frantic as Father is over Marley. It was an antique diamond bracelet!"

"Damn, I should have asked more for it!"

"You sold it? One of the crown jewels of Laitmea, to fund your debauchery?"

Kestly shrugged, unapologetic.

"Add that to the list of things the King and Queen will find out about if you don't help us," said Jessimin.

"Ah, now we get to the meat of the issue. I know you have some of my little secrets, what is it that you want for them?" She brushed out her waist length blonde hair, nudging the last sapphire pin that fell out under the table with her toe.

"We're going to be gone for a while. A week, maybe longer, planning Pippy's ball. We need you to watch Redgie. Follow him everywhere, note anything suspicious he might do. Don't let him know that you're watching, don't let him know that we know anything. Just make sure that he's never alone. We don't know what he might try, so you'll have to be alert. We only know that he's plotting something, and that it could result in death if he has a chance to see it through."

Kestly nodded.

"A week without parties, meeting friends, anything like that. A week or more of tracking my own big brother. I suppose that's better than I would get if everyone read Tobias' letters. Fair enough, I will watch him like a hawk, and report him immediately if I suspect that someone is in danger. But be warned, this is the only thing you'll get out of me. You can't rework the bargain now. You leave, and you forget you ever read that letter. If you try to use it against me again, I'll find a way to make your lives more miserable than you could possibly imagine."

"Deal," said Jessimin.

"Deal," said Pippy.

"I suppose that's reasonable," said Mayzin, and shook Kestly's hand.

* * *

KESTLY

Veena

In all my descriptions of kings and histories of our people, I never wrote an account of Carsten. It was a gross oversight on my uncle's part, as there has hardly been a more crucial player in our plan. Carsten is not of any noble heritage, but was born to two pirates of the First Order. He is handsome, strong, and well-built. He is my one true love, my Uncle's killer, and my deputy leader of the Third Order. He obeys my orders without any question. One could not buy such loyalty.

He has grown up among the raiding parties, and is one of our most adept warriors and tacticians. He has also provided a lovely solution to the problem of the prince and the nomad girl.

They appear to have escaped. Marley actually did, briefly, but we caught him listening to our plans. I'm not sure how much he knows, but I am sure that he could do substantial damage if Zavaxer released him back to Laitmea. He could also upend my plans if he spoke to Zavaxer, seeing as he knows that I am not loyal to the First Order. I have had a hard time convincing him to trust me again as things stand. As little as he trusts the prince, Marley could still wreck my good name and have Zavaxer lock Carsten and me in a cell instead.

However, Carsten had his men bring Marley and Katjia to Death's Cliff Bluff, where we loaded them onto a smaller boat. Carsten was able to return to the cove in enough time to sound the alarm through the morning air, as if they had just escaped their cell. Nobody will wonder why I am missing, as I have been pacing for hours in the night, lamenting my fall from grace with the king. I will be taking them shortly to the outer reaches of the archipelago, and leaving them on an island with a population of dragons. No matter how anyone searches, they'll never find a corpse where a dragon lives.

I will return and volunteer my services in tracking them down. Zavaxer is not so angry at me that he will deny me a chance to prove my loyalty again. This will provide just the opportunity that Carsten and I need to set the final stage of our plot in motion.

When all is said and done, Carsten will lead the United Order of Pirates, and I shall be his Queen. This record will indeed be counted among our greatest triumphs.

Redgenold wrote me yesterday to say that the assassination attempts will be made soon, and that he is ready to command the men of the Third Order in his coup. My informant has written to me to let me know that the suitable candidate is also ready to assume command, not of our motley assortment of mercenaries, but of the country.

I need to set this account aside and prepare myself to row our prisoners to their fate, but ah, it is wondrous to see all of my plans come together so beautifully. I think that my first act after the fighting ends will be to ask Carsten to marry me. Partly for love, and partly because he can become arrogant, and will need to be reminded who made him King of the Pirates.

* * *

Marley

I could have escaped, but now I'm in a holding cell again. Last evening, Carsten came in to taunt us and give us fresh water and a loaf of bread.

He probably would have stayed for several minutes, but just then Veena called him quite urgently. What she needed him for was unclear, but I was sure that it wasn't romantic in nature. No, I had seen how they behaved together after her uncle's demise, and those irate shrieks could not possibly be signaling another moonlit kiss. My immediate guess was that something of their clandestine chicanery had been discovered by King Zavaxer or his men. Whatever they were plotting, it was not with the King's blessing. I suspected that they might even be intending to replace him.

Whatever the case, Carsten left in such a hurry that he didn't lock the door quite securely behind him. I knew that I ought to point this out to Katjia and plan a daring escape, but I wanted to know what Veena and Carsten were up to, and I knew that Katjia wouldn't approve of what I had in mind. Besides, I thought that I could come back after I was done snooping and let her go. Well, if anyone reads this, I'm sure they'll know how this episode turned out.

As soon as Katjia fell asleep, I slid outside. I saw that we were being kept in one of the few actual buildings in Pirate's Cove. The door opened directly onto the path to the dock. This, according to Veena, was the domain of the Second Order of pirates—the medics, cooks, young and infirm. There was no night patrol. Clearly, the pirates thought themselves very safe within their

128

inner sanctum.

There was only one pirate ship moored in the bay. It was a beautiful beast. Sixty oarsmen would propel it when maximum speed was necessary. Fifteen knots, perhaps. There were two quilted sails, and a rear oar, instead of a rudder. This ship could go backwards just as soon as forwards, judging by the shape of the prow. There was only one deck, but the mizzenmast had a small crow's nest.

As I drew closer, I saw that the lapped wood was painted with tar, and unusually, a red dye. The red swirls and vines and dragons made it a terrifying sight indeed. Carsten has said that they pack the chinks with otter fur for extra protection. Even with my heart thumping in my chest, I couldn't help but admire the craftsmanship that had clearly gone into this battle-ready beauty.

I decided that it couldn't hurt to look a little closer. The ship floated in only a few feet of water, so walking along the shore, I could get a very good view of it. I waded out into the water until I stood directly in front of it. The sea was ice cold, and I felt my legs going numb after only a few minutes, so I hauled myself up a ways on one of the ropes. It was far harder than the deckhands back in Lyrah made it look. My arms were soon burning just as much as my legs were freezing. Then, as I hung just below the deck of the ship, I heard Veena and Carsten talking. They were less than a yard away, and all they would need to do was look over the edge of the ship, and they would see me.

As I had hoped, they were discussing their plot against Zavaxer. It seems that they are part of an order of pirates heretofore unknown to me, called the Third Order. Personally, I think they need to work out a better name for themselves. If their goal is to strike fear into the hearts of their adversaries, the Third Order isn't going to do the job. I would go with something more along the lines of The Blood Dragons, or the King-Slayers, but that is neither here nor there.

Veena was waxing eloquent about how Katjia and I had done nothing but hinder her plans. Much of her and Carsten's conversation was dominated by mumbled epithets and likely kisses, and I gathered that he was comforting her.

As I suspected, something of their plans had come to the attention of the King. He was upset that Laitmea had not received his offer to peaceably return us, and was very unhappy with Veena for allowing the "hostage situation" to persist for as long as it has. Actually, I'm not sure how long exactly it's been. A week? Ten days? Being locked in a windowless room has destroyed my perception of the passing of time.

King Zavaxer thinks that Veena wants to provoke war between our countries, which is not far off the mark. He's talking about stripping her of much of her responsibility. But Veena doesn't just want to kill Katjia and myself. She wants to replace the whole royal family. She has an informant in the nobility, who has a new King set to take the throne if the Third Order removes my family. I nearly fell back into the water when I heard that. I've been trying to come to terms with being killed myself, but she would kill us all! Mayzin and Jessimin and everyone. I can't let that happen! Not that there's much I can do about it.

She leads the Third Order with Carsten, and she's going to send them to attack the palace. Either my ears stopped working from shock, or she and Carsten spent a long time kissing after that proclamation, for it was minutes before I heard her say things about how her Uncle used to lead the order. I already knew that he hadn't faithfully represented his king's wishes to Aunty Trill and Uncle Dowlin, so that wasn't much of a surprise. I did learn that she had killed him and taken over the Third Order because her Uncle hadn't used his skills as a medic to save her mother, and she had grown up as an orphan because of him. Otherwise, he wanted the same things that she does: Laitmean governance that allows the pirates to steal our ships and our people.

I know that mother and Aunty Trill *were* pirates once, but that was when Haputa and Laitmea were at war, and Darin the Terrible was still alive. Things were different then. Now, the pirates aren't opposing an unjust regime, they're threatening hard-won peace. I was so disgusted by everything Veena said that I almost missed Carsten saying:

"Vee-Vee, it doesn't matter if he knows. We're putting the plan in action tomorrow, and soon enough everyone will see that the Third Order has done right by the pirates. Zavaxer will be thrown out as soon as your puppet Redgenold fulfills his duty."

Redge! I can only assume that he meant my brother and not my father, because father would never be a puppet of Veena's. They're having Redgie try to kill the rest of my family and sow chaos so they can put their own government in place. That would also explain why I saw Veena and Redge dancing at the ball. She was seducing him to use in her plot!

Then Carsten said, "We only need to make it look like the prisoners have escaped on their own. That way, nobody will suspect us, and Zavaxer can spend his last days as King happy that he has an excuse to give Laitmea."

Veena said, "I don't care whether or not he's happy. I just care that he doesn't interfere this close to the end. The fighting will last at least a week, and I will need to return to the capital to see that it all goes smoothly. Until it's all said and done, I won't rest easy."

They were talking about me and Katjia. My arms were aching, and even the terror coursing through me wasn't keeping me warm after wading in the frigid bay. The last thing I heard Carsten say before I fell was,

"Don't leave bodies for them to find. The last thing we need is Zavaxer onto us when we're both away in Laitmea."

It was far too much to hope that they didn't hear the splash, of course. It was so cold that I was almost glad when they pulled me out of the depths and onto the boat. Almost.

Veena demanded to know how much I had overheard, then said that it didn't matter anyway, because she had already decided what she was going to do with me. She had Carsten fetch a few oarsmen to man the ship, and then, to my horror, he brought Katjia out of the cell. I wanted to tell her everything I had overheard, but I couldn't, not without letting her know that I chose to chase Veena rather than escape when I could have.

I just sat there in shocked silence while Veena took us to the nearest island in the Archipelago of Doom, Death's Cliff Bluff. She gave us our meager belongings back, and as dawn broke she loaded us into a small rowboat from the pirate outpost there, and left Carsten to get the ship back to the mainland.

She's been rowing for over an hour now. I don't know where we're being taken, but my guess is that it's worse than where we were.

* * *

Katjia

"How are we going to get off of this island?" Marley screamed, looking desperately after Veena's departing rowboat.

"Make a boat?" Katjia suggested, not nearly so perturbed by their predicament. "You must know enough about ship craft to see us back to Mer."

"We'd need rope, and a saw, and goodness knows the currents in the bay are strong enough. The best we could hope for without any proper tools would be a raft, and that might only get us to the next island before it fell apart. That's right back into pirate territory, in case you're wondering. We'll never get back to the mainland!" The salt spray had plastered Marley's hair to his head, and he now bore a striking resemblance to a bedraggled kitten. He seemed about to cry.

"Oh, don't whine. It was only my first thought. We've got days left yet before we starve, and there's rainwater to drink. It might not be the most pleasant time, but we're not fools. I'm certain we'll find a way off this dratted rock before we die."

The more time Katjia spent with the young prince, the more she realized how inexperienced he was. His entire life had been spent in book learning. While she had been learning how to cook meals, ride horses, and if need be, fight with a staff, he had been happily ensconced in the palace, coloring pictures of ships. It was likely that encountering Veena had been the first real danger he had ever known.

She had understood in an abstract way that Marley didn't really have practical skills, but it hadn't mattered much when they were being held hostage by pirates. Now, however, his fearful attitude made much more sense. He wasn't trying to be annoying, he was trying to cope, and he didn't have the first idea where to begin.

"I know you wanted a story-book adventure, Marley, but you're getting a real one," she said, pacing back and forth on the shore, taking inventory. Veena had mercifully left her pack, with its ever-dwindling supply of flatbread and mare's milk cheese. Better than nothing.

Marley really was crying now, and she decided to leave him be for a while to sort out his feelings. She skirted the edge of the dense forest, wary of getting lost. She was happy to find a hefty tree branch that could serve as a makeshift staff, and a goodly supply of dry wood. Whether the jungle would yield anything edible remained to be seen. The beach was composed mainly of thumb-sized pebbles, but she found enough larger rocks to build a crude ring, and she promptly set about building a fire. The islands might be more temperate than Mer itself, but night was fast approaching, and there was no point in freezing to death.

By the time the sun was touching the horizon, she had a merrily roaring blaze and a pile of wood to last the night. She hung her cloak and blankets on a branch just close enough to the flames to dry them, and laid out the last of her rations in orderly piles, before calling down the shore.

"Dinner!"

Marley unfolded himself from the rock he had been hunched on and crunched towards her. His eyes were still rimmed with read, but he seemed to have regained most of his composure. He crouched next to the fire, and ate his allotted portion of bread and cheese without complaint.

"I'm sorry if I've been sharp with you," Katjia began, once they were full. "This whole misadventure has made me a little tense."

Much to her relief, he managed a weak chuckle. In the warm light of the fire, he looked almost handsome.

"You've been wonderful. I'm sorry I'm so useless," he said, meeting her gaze for the first time. His eyes were as green as grass. Katjia's stomach felt like it was trying to turn over inside of her at the sight. Her breath caught in her chest, and it took her a moment to realize that he was still talking.

"I don't know how to start a fire or fight off bandits or escape from pirates... or talk to girls..."

"You're talking to me," she said weakly. "Maybe being stuck on this island isn't such a bad thing after all."

Marley flushed as red as the sunset.

"It's not just us I'm worried about," he said, after a while. "Before Veena rowed us out here for dead, I overheard her and Carsten talking. They lied to us about the accord with Laitmea."

"I didn't think they were being honest, what with the fact that we were their prisoners. They must have been right in the king's inner circle, or they wouldn't have been in charge of hostages. What did they really know?"

"They were working against King Zavaxer. He really did want to negotiate a deal with my parents and the king. Vee and Carsten lead some group called the Third Order. The diplomat was part of it too, before they had him killed. The accord was all a sham so that Vee could contact somebody in Laitmea to have the government overthrown. They don't want peace, they want a whole new royal family."

Katjia sucked in a sharp breath. "So your whole family is in danger from this Third Order, then."

Marley nodded miserably. "They could be attacking as we speak. There's not enough of them to overwhelm the whole of Lyrah, but they have someone on the inside."

"How are they going to put somebody on the throne, though? They can't wipe out all the royalty."

"They want to get inside the keep. If there's fighting, Dart will be away defending Aunt Trill and they can steal all sorts of secret documents that would bring down the monarchy."

"And who would rule instead?"

"They didn't say."

Katjia watched the waves rolling in for a while, thinking. "Well, that settles it. We'll just need to find a way off this island, warn everyone at the palace, and get those documents first. The Third Order will be in for a surprise when they reach the capital."

"How, though? Unless something's changed that I haven't noticed?"

"I was hoping you'd thought of something."

"Only that we should explore the forest, but that's not guaranteed to get us anywhere." Marley stared glumly into the fire.

"Either way, we can't do anything in the dark. Lets get some sleep," Katjia said, pulling her cloak off its branch and curling up under it. "You can have the blanket."

If he replied, she didn't hear him, for almost as soon as her head touched the rocky ground, she was asleep.

* * *

Marley

I don't think I could bear if Katjia knew that I'm the one responsible for getting us stuck on this godforsaken rock. Alright, I'm getting ahead of myself. I forgot to say where it was that Vee took us.

She bundled the both of us into a rowboat, and spent the better part of the day rowing us out to the most barren and isolated islet in the archipelago. It makes sense. If she had just killed us in the cove, the other pirates would have found the bodies, and hers and Carsten's plot would have been uncovered. This way, when we starve to death, no one will be the wiser. It looks to all the world like my escape was successful, and that is exactly what Vee wants.

I don't know what Carsten sees in that girl. She's pretty, I guess, with all that corn-floss yellow hair, but the look in her eyes is just chilling. I like Katjia much better. She might not be considered a classic beauty, but she's got a nice enough face and she's about a thousand times nicer. I just wish she weren't so intimidating.

Fortunately, Vee gave her all her things back except for her staff. If anyone can figure out how to get us out of this predicament, it's her. But as I began, I don't want her to know why Vee decided to put us here. I feel like a dishonest cheat for not coming clean, but if she knows that I was caught spying, she'd probably hate me, and I just couldn't bear it.

I wish I were better at talking to people. Mayzin is good at that. Katjia's better with the practical things—fighting, setting up camp, getting food. I'm no good at either. I'm as useless as a nomad as I am a noble. Self deprecating, I know, but I have gotten us into this mess, after all, and I've done nothing to help except stay out of Katjia's way and cry on a rock. For all my love of ships, I can't even get us off this island. I have to say, a little river sailing is far preferable to the open ocean after all. I've spent so long dreaming of pirate ships, I suppose it stands to reason that I have a miserable time in them. If the feeling in the pit of my stomach weren't guilt, I'd definitely call it seasickness.

Katjia's calling me for dinner now, I suppose I will have to continue this maudlin rant later.

* * *

Katjia

Morning on the island was freezing. The salty sea still roiled and frothed in the distance, but the mud flats left by the receding tide were flecked with frost. The fire had burned itself down to a low bed of coals, which Katjia and Marley huddled over for warmth. Katjia broke pieces of a frozen puddle into her empty canteen, and hung it on the branch above the fire to melt. The next-to-last piles of bread and cheese sat like lead in their stomachs.

Katjia kept her cloak wrapped tightly around herself, while Marley made do with the blanket. Steely clouds had blown in overnight, lending the world a grayish cast even when the sun was fully up. By mid-morning, it was a little warmer, but not much.

"I don't know if there's anything to find on this island," Marley said, as Katjia rose and put out the fire.

"And we can't know until we look," she replied, re-packing her bag. "Carry this, won't you?" She tossed him the pack and hefted her makeshift staff. "I'm the only one who's handy with a weapon, and if we find anything dangerous I want to have both hands free."

He shouldered it, looking only slightly aggrieved and followed her into the damp dark of the forest.

There were no trails on the island, nor any signs of habitation. Katjia was careful to mark the ground with the butt of her staff every few paces, so that they would be able to find their way back to the shore. There was an eerie silence under the trees. The sound of the ocean faded into the distance, leaving only a few insects humming and Marley's steady breathing behind. There was no birdsong.

Katjia shivered, though forcing her way through the underbrush had made her much warmer. "Do you know what this island is called?" she asked, noting that they were traveling slowly but steadily uphill.

"There's lots of little islands in the archipelago," Marley replied in a hushed tone, seeming even more disturbed by the silence than she was. "Most of them don't have names." He paused for a moment to consider. "This one's a little bigger than I initially thought, though. Let's see… we were on Death's Cliff Bluff, and we've come further east, so that would make this… The Tooth."

"Not a pleasant name," she said.

"No, not pleasant at all," he agreed.

A while later, they came to a much steeper rise. It took nearly an hour to scale, and by the time they reached the top, they were both panting. The whole of the island was spread out below them.

"It must be nearly forty miles across at the widest point," Marley said, "and maybe ten miles long, all of it jungle."

Katjia had to agree that the vista was less than pleasing. Aside from a faint rocky boarder, the island was nothing but green. They had an endless supply of wood, but not much else. "Well, that's that. Let's get back down to the beach and try to think of something else," she sighed. They had not taken more than ten paces, however, when she threw up her hand to stop Marley.

"Look."

There, pressed deep into the mud, was a set of tracks. Gargantuan, four-clawed tracks, almost as wide as her staff.

Marley let out a weak moan. "A dragon lives here. We've been wandering around an island with a giant man-eating lizard. Veena must have thought that it could use a snack."

Katjia ignored him. An idea was forming in her mind. A wild, improbable idea that might just work.

"Doesn't your Aunty Trill ride a dragon?" she asked, starting to follow the tracks. Marley grabbed her by the back of her cloak.

"No! No, Katjia, NO!"

She raised an eyebrow at him. "Have you got a better idea?"

"I've got an idea that I'd like to stay alive! Aunty Trill and my mum stole Dart from his nest when he was a *baby*. You can't go ride a fully grown dragon. They need to be trained, and even then it's dangerous!"

"Have you got a better idea?"

"It's a wild animal! Those tracks look bigger than Dart's. It must be fifty or sixty years old at least. We'd die trying to get anywhere near it!"

"And we'll also die if we stay here until our food runs out. *Have you got a better idea!*"

"No… but Katjia, please don't make me do this."

"You can wait here." She said caustically, striding back under the trees.

"That's even worse!" he shouted, running after her. "If I'm going to die, I don't want to do it alone."

The far side of the rise bore clear signs of the island's fire-breathing resident. The tracks they followed were clearly a trail, along which smaller trees had been knocked down to make more room. Here and there, sun-bleached shed scales lay in the mud, and there was a faint but noticeable brimstone smell to the air. It now made sense that there was no birdsong.

Katjia thought that Marley was going to lose his nerve when they came upon a heap of deer bones, but he only turned a little green and mumbled a few curse words.

Then she saw it. The dragon was curled up on a rocky outcropping that rose above the trees, carefully licking the inside of its leg. It was enormous, far bigger than Dart, and violently purple. Like the queen's dragon, it had fierce orange eyes, but its horns, spikes, and wings were also orange. Beneath the outcropping lay a more recently killed deer.

"Marley," she whispered, reaching behind her to clasp his sweaty hand, "You may have been absolutely right."

"At least it's not hungry," he whispered back. His hand was shaking.

"Fine time to develop a sense of humor," she huffed. "Alright, it's just a horse. A very big horse, with a lot of sharp teeth. Just a horse." She marched up to the outcropping. The dragon raised its head and uttered a soft growl.

Up close, it was even more terrifying.

"Hello, dragon, would you mind very much if we rode you back to Laitmea? You seem to be the only way off this island," she said.

The growling intensified.

"It doesn't understand you," said Marley, "The only reason it hasn't attacked yet is because everything usually runs away from it. It thinks you might be a threat."

"That's good, right?"

"Not really. Dragons only fly away from threats that are bigger than them."

"And threats that are smaller than them?"

"That's what the fire is for."

"Oh."

The dragon cocked its head at them, seeming confused. The growling quieted, but did not stop. It began to lash its enormous tail back and forth. Katjia braced for it to pounce, but it didn't.

"Why aren't we dead?" she asked, turning to Marley.

He was frowning, but as she watched, comprehension dawned on his face. "It wants your staff."

She gaped at him, and lifted the branch. The dragon followed the movement intently.

"Throw it," he said. Without questioning, she obliged, hurling the staff off the outcropping into the trees below.

The dragon let out a deafening roar and dove after it, fanning out its massive wings.

"Shall we run for it?" she asked, relieved.

"Lets," said Marley.

They bolted back the way they had come, not stopping until they were back on the beach, gasping for air.

"This day just keeps getting better and better," Marley said bitterly. The sun was sinking again, and they were no closer to leaving.

Just as they were about to restart the fire, however, a roar sounded nearby. The huge purple dragon came skidding out of the underbrush, Katjia's staff clamped between its jaws. It roared again and pranced over to their hastily

142

set up camp. It dropped the branch at Katjia's feet, and sat down expectantly, tail wagging. Marley slapped his own face. "Dragons love to play fetch," he said.

Katjia took the now slimy staff and lobbed it down the beach. The dragon bounded after it, roaring all the while.

"You keep it occupied while I start the fire," she said, leaving the bewildered Marley to play fetch.

By the time their meager dinner was ready, the dragon was sprawled out on the beach, gnawing on an uprooted tree, its sides heaving.

"It won't stay friendly forever," Marley cautioned, wolfing down his bread with dragon-spittle-covered hands.

"I don't know," Katjia mused, eating her own food more slowly.

Marley shrugged, throwing his cheese towards the dragon. It looked up just in time to catch the morsel in its jaws and the cheese vanished down its gullet.

Stretching like a cat, the dragon rose and padded up to the fire. Though it had as yet shown no inclination to eat them, the pair couldn't help but shy away from the great purple head. It gently nosed Katjia, nearly knocking her over.

"I think it wants more," said Marley, and Katjia proffered her own cheese. The dragon caught the cheese on the end of its barbed tongue and ate it, then prodded Marley with its fore-paw, sending him sprawling across the beach.

"I don't have any more!" he shouted, once he had regained his breath. The dragon swung its head around and sniffed him from head to toe, and finding that he was, in fact, out of cheese, it began to whine.

Never one to miss an opportunity, Katjia rose and tapped the dragon on its flank.

"Dragon, there's more cheese that way," she said, pointing toward the mainland. It stopped whining, and stared at her with one orange eye.

"We can show you where to get more cheese," she said slowly. Though her words could not have made sense to the beast, it seemed to understand her general intent, for it stiffened, and stared longingly at the distant shore.

"Marley," she said quietly, "We have to get on its back now, before it changes its mind."

It was a testament to how desperately he wanted to reach his family in time that Marley did not protest. He flung himself onto the dragon's tail and scrambled up its scaly back and over its wings until he straddled its neck. He reached down and pulled Katjia up in front of him with a grunt. Katjia kicked the dragon and pointed across the water.

"More cheese, that way!" she shouted, and the dragon furled its wings. Marley gripped Katjia tightly around the waist and closed his eyes. The dragon took off, hurtling through the air at a frightening speed. Marley couldn't even scream, but as they flew into the sunset sky, he heard Katjia yell, "I don't want to die alone either!"

* * *

THE TOOTH

Kanara

Kanara did not like the man in black. It was an instantaneous, visceral hatred that transcended all rational thought.

A man in dark tunic and tights was a common sight in the rear courtyard of the palace, as was a woman in the same dress. It was, after all, standard servant garb on days when no special duty was required. Kanara had seen so many black-clad men come and go over the past weeks that he had stopped bothering to learn their names.

So then.

He shouldn't be alarmed by the sight of one more unnamed servant, even if he didn't recall this one's face. The palace was a large place; it was more than conceivable that there were a dozen servants he had never seen before. But even as these thoughts presented themselves, he slipped into the shadows and began to follow the man.

In his heart, he knew. That feeling that swelled inside him was recognition, not of the face but of the gait and the movement of the hands. He hated this man on sight, because he moved like one who is out to kill. He hated this man on sight, because he wore the same look as the man who had taken away Gynn.

Kanara could move softly when he wanted to. It was a common enough skill, something any good hunter could do, but it was always shocking to glimpse him on tiptoe. A bulk such as his should not have been capable of stealth.

His quarry never noticed him, but his quarry did not act as someone who expected to be followed. He moved about the palace with the familiarity of a long time servant, and for a moment, Kanara was struck by the ridiculous notion that if he could not keep the man in his sights, he would be hopelessly lost within the maze of corridors.

Just when he began to wonder if his suspicions were wrong, if he was tracking a harmless footman, Kanara sensed a change. Suddenly his prey was acting like prey, glancing left and right, scurrying between shadows, and, to his horror, pulling a shiny wood and metal object from the black tunic.

Gun. That was what it was. Surprising that he recalled the name, but anyone could see its deadly nature. It was so different from the Lords' hunting blunderbusses, he wondered why the two instruments shared a name. Then he wondered what in Eretz he was doing, completely unarmed, following a man who had a gun, or four, by the bulge of his tunic. But what else was there to do? If he tried to sound the alarm, he'd surely be shot at. If he ran, if he could find someone. If he didn't get lost, somebody else could be shot at by then, and taken away like Gynn. If he continued to follow…

Use your head, stupid boy. But wasn't it too late for that? If he had used his head at all, it should have been to sound the alarm when he first saw the suspicious man. Now that he'd failed to do that, wasn't it all the same if he kept *not* using his head?

Father had always used his head. *And he wound up dead just like all the rest of them. Katjia is right. I don't have to be just like father. As long as I try my hardest to lead us well, I won't be a failure.*

The man in black stopped before a door, a highly polished, well appointed-door that looked grand and expensive even in a palace. If this wasn't the living quarters of someone important, Kanara would eat his own boot. And if this man wasn't here to kill that someone important, he'd eat the pair.

By the time the man had worked the lock open, Kanara had made up his mind to stop him no matter what, and so he stopped being stealthy and made a dash for it. Through the door he went, just as the man paused and took aim. Kanara crashed into the black-clad assassin, bearing him to the floor, hoping beyond hope that the cataclysmic bang of the gun had not signaled the demise of the *someone important.* Ripping the smoking instrument from its wielder's hand, Kanara smacked him over the head with his own gun.

"Weapon of the future it may be," he grunted, hurling it aside and flipping the man onto his back. "It could do with some improvement." He thought the man was unconscious, but gave him a few good punches to be sure.

Then he looked up to see the intended victim of the attack: a young woman, with caramel-colored curls that fell to her waist and eyes of honey brown. Her dress was pale gold, as was the tiara on her head.

"Are you quite well, eh, Princess Addmaleta?"

"Yes," she said, then, just as quickly, "no." And she swooned into Kanara's arms.

* * *

Mayzin

We're on the river to Aunty Ettalara's. We had an easy time convincing mother to let us go, given how she hates parties and almost forgot that Pippy will be of age very shortly. I don't think I'll have eight children, myself. I want to be able to keep track of all of my offspring.

It was also pretty simple to blackmail Kestly into watching Redge for us, which I almost worry about. She's far to blasé about things that should be important. She really ought to be courting someone, or married, but no. She's still flirting with half a dozen boys, staying out till all hours of the night, and stealing to support herself. Aunty Trill is supposed to be the only kleptomaniac in the family. She's not even a blood relative, so I don't see how Kestly could take after her.

We'll have to have another chat with her when we return. Mother certainly isn't going to intervene for Kessie's own good. Even if she doesn't want to find a nice boy and settle down, it would still do her good to spend less time in a dockside tavern. Pippy's been writing to Duke Javis' son, too. At this rate, even Jessimin will have a husband before Kestly.

I'm feeling a little seasick, so I think I'll put this away and write any more updates when we arrive. There will be a carriage waiting for us at Firdell, so it really won't be very long to get there.

* * *

Kanara

Kanara was nonplussed.

It was clear from even a cursory inspection that the princess was not injured. There was no blood, no telltale hole in her dress. The would-be assassin had missed by a mile, taking a large chunk out of the headboard of a very fine bed. There was no reason at all, he decided, for her to collapse, unless one counted his own arrival.

If one was accustomed to a pampered palace life, he supposed, then the sudden arrival of a man intent on killing you, swiftly followed by a large tribesman *might* be shock enough to induce a faint, but he really wasn't sure. Maybe it had more to do with the overly tight bodice of her dress. He briefly considered loosening it for her, then decided that however tight it might be, she was a foreigner and would likely take offense when she woke.

Under other circumstances, he would assume her to be suffering heat stroke, but her room was cool and well ventilated. There was a half-emptied glass of cider on her table, so she wasn't dehydrated either. At last, having exhausted all other explanations, he put her state down to shock alone, and moved to place her onto her bed.

She really was a very pretty creature, he decided.

Her head lolled against his chest as he lifted her, and her eyelids fluttered open for a moment.

"Oh, dear," she mumbled, "this is really happening isn't it?"

He set her down gently among the frilly cushions and embroidered pillows and smoothed back her hair.

"There was a man trying to shoot me!" She tried to sit up the moment he stepped away, but promptly fell back with a second, "Oh, dear."

Even if Kanara had come up with a plan in the first place, he was sure it would not have encompassed anything after protecting the princess from immediate harm.

"Shall I fetch someone for you, princess?"

Please, he wished, *please direct me to someone who has some idea of how to deal with this. Princesses are only supposed to exist in fairy stories. And they're not supposed to swoon.*

She did not answer his question.

She had managed to roll herself about in bed, and was looking at the man sprawled on the floor, clutching a pillow to her chest.

"Really!" She exclaimed with an indignant huff. "All my life I've wondered what I would do in the face of real danger, and now there's a man with a loaded gun in my bedchamber, and all I can do is faint and feel weak at the knees. This is entirely my mother's fault."

"The queen is trying to kill you?" Kanara exclaimed, eyes widening.

"No, no. I don't mean that she's responsible for his presence," She gestured at the man, "I have no idea who sent him. I mean that it's my mother's fault that I don't know how to handle myself in a dangerous situation. She fought in battles and chased away bandits when she was younger than I am now, but she is *convinced* that I have a better life being a pampered pet. Just look at me, falling into the arms of a strange man. It's a disgrace! Well, perhaps this will make her see the light and let me have some knives or a sword or something." She looked up at him, an almost childish look of triumph in her eyes.

"Who are you, anyway?"

"Kanara, princess."

"Oh, one of the nomads. Well, thank goodness my idiot cousin invited your family to stay. Who knows what would have happened otherwise. I'm very sorry that you had to catch me, but your appearance was a little, well, sudden."

"At least it was only shock. I was afraid for a moment that your dress had suffocated you."

"Oh, It certainly was a contributing factor. You could have unlaced the corset, you know. That always helps bring a Lady around."

Kanara was becoming distinctly uncomfortable. The princess was so... forward. So utterly unconcerned by his presence.

"I really ought to find someone. An attempt has been made on your life. One can only assume that your entire family is in danger, the alarm must be sounded."

"No, please don't leave. Disgrace it might be, but I don't think I'd feel entirely safe, alone with that man, even if he is incapacitated. Do you mind?"

"Then how-"

"Leave it to me."

The princess lifted herself into a sitting position, and began to shout at the top of her lungs.

"Help, help! There's an unconscious man in my chambers who needs to be removed immediately. I'm quite alright, but it would probably be best to sound an alarm anyway. Either way, the man has to go, so snap to it! Help!"

Thunderous footsteps came almost immediately, and in a matter of moments, the door was opened by a half dozen out-of-breath servants.

"Quite a verbose cry for help, princess Addmaleta," the lead man exclaimed, "And there are two men in here!"

"Yes, Bernard, but you can leave the handsome one. He saved my life. It's just the unconscious assassin that needs to be disposed of, thank you very much."

Kanara wished he could turn invisible, like a magic man in a story. *Handsome one?*

Bernard's eyebrows swiftly shot up. "I'm afraid, princess, that this is *very much* out of my hands." He said, "I shall inform the king and queen directly."

* * *

Mayzin

This afternoon, we arrived at Aunty Ettalara's. It's been a few years since I've been here, and I'd forgotten how stuffy it is. She's fond of collecting dainty little trinkets and stashing them on every free surface.

I always thought Aunty was the most grown up of the adults in our family, but I can almost see what mother means when she calls her prissy or uptight. I've always been the most comfortable with royal goings on of any of us, so I don't find being here too bad, but poor Jessimin is having a time of it. She's always preferred climbing trees and playing with Dart to staying inside, but here, even outside is just as perfectly manicured as everything else.

We've told her our suspicions regarding Redge, and thus far, she seems to be taking us seriously. She said that it will be safest for us to remain here and pretend that things are going on as normal, and she sent several letters, which she assured us were to people who could help. I'm sure she'll have worded them vaguely enough that Redge won't be able to catch on that we know anything, but still, that makes me nervous.

Ettalara entertained us for dinner, but left us on our own for desert, so she could attend to other matters. I'm grateful that she's helping us, but I do think it would have been nice of her to tell us exactly what she's doing. We deserve to know, given that we were the ones that told her.

* * *

Kanara

Bernard issued a series of commands, and in only a few moments, Kanara was being led down the hall by a group of palace guards, a second group dragging the assassin behind them. Bernard, it seemed, was the chief palace butler, in charge of all servants save the royal family's personal staff. He walked ahead of the strange procession, escorting the princess, who was still slightly unsteady on her feet. He also carried the gun, resting on a silver tray probably meant for letters and cards. The whole event was becoming utterly surreal.

Kanara hoped that they wouldn't be brought into the throne room, where all the lords and ladies could gawk at him and whisper about what had happened. At least, he assumed they would whisper. Perhaps the stories were wrong, and the nobles of Laitmea were so unabashed about their gossip that they would shout their speculations to the world. Which would be even worse. Realizing that his thoughts were in total disarray, Kanara attempted to steady himself, and was much relieved when they came upon a small and private space.

The private audience hall was just as richly decorated as the rest of the palace, but it had a lived in quality that Kanara found comfortingly similar to his own tent.

There were only four people already present. Bernard announced their titles, but there was no need. The king and queen sat resplendent on matching thrones, looking as stern and disapproving as one would expect. The king, dark haired and richly dressed, had eyes precisely the same shade of brown as the princesses, but with a cold and ruthless edge that made Kanara even more uncomfortable than he already was.

The queen too, seemed dangerous, but in a different way. Everyone knew that she had been a pickpocket in her younger days, and Kanara doubted very much that her skills had grown rusty since her ascension to the throne. Her caramel hair might have been done up in a sophisticated style under her crown, her dress might have been arranged neatly about her, but in *her* sea-green eyes, Kanara saw still the grit and determination of the thieving orphan.

It was a moment before he could spare any attention for the others. The royals' personal guards stood in the shadows behind their respective thrones, dressed neither as members of the court nor as servants, but in plain and practical clothes. Behind the king must have been Lord Captain of the Guard Redgenold, at his ease in black velvet with only the finest trim of gold. If he was alarmed, he did not show it. He only chewed on the end of his mustache thoughtfully.

Behind the queen, was her lady-in-waiting, princess Quipeneay, openly haughty and unconcerned. They said she always wore red to hide the stains of blood from those who tried to hurt the queen. Perhaps she was mad, perhaps only loyal to a fault. Either way, Kanara suspected that if anyone in the room was going to kill him, it would be Quipeneay.

* * *

PRINCESS
ADDMALETA

Marley

I'm back in Lyrah, of all places. It's been a few days, I know, but this is the first time that my hands haven't been shaking too badly to write. We were only stranded on The Tooth for a day, but it was the most harrowing day of my life, and it was swiftly followed by the most harrowing *night* of my life, for Katjia and I escaped upon the back of a fully grown dragon.

The beast is larger than Dart, and perhaps twice as ferocious. The only reason it afforded us safe passage was because it has an affinity for cheese. An adult dragon has never been tamed before, so perhaps I should consider myself lucky to have witnessed such a remarkable event, but riding a dragon is not the wondrous experience Aunty Trill makes it out to be.

I was screaming bloody murder in Katjia's ear the whole time we were over the ocean. I'd apologize, but she was so terrified herself that I don't think she heard me. It wasn't much better over land. We were able to point the beast in the right direction by the stars and made good time, but the dragon's neck pitched up and down with every flap of its wings, so by the time dawn came we had both thrown up whatever was left of our dinners. We arrived at the capital by mid-afternoon, well ahead of any pirate attack. Even if the Third Order set their plans in motion the moment Vee returned from The Tooth, they still won't be at the capital for at least another few days.

The first thing we did upon landing was find the closest butcher's shop and beg two wheels of cheese from the owner. After eating them both, the dragon was happy to follow us to the palace gates, and there, things became interesting. Dart was sleeping on the outer parapet, and when he woke and saw the great purple beast, he went wild. I don't think he's seen another dragon since he was stolen from his nest as a day-old hatchling, and at first, I thought he didn't know how to behave.

Normally, he just sniffs newcomers and lets them pass with a wag of his tail, but this time, he jumped down, nearly crushing a building in the process, and started to do some kind of bizarre dance, with his wings fully flared over his head like a strange hat. When our dragon responded to his wild roaring, however, it became immediately clear that she was a female, and Dart was issuing some kind of mating call.

By the time the noise drew the palace guards to investigate, the two were high in the sky, flapping in circles and screaming at each other. Anyway, we've named the purple one Eldrid, and there are now two dragons roosting on the roof.

I had hoped that this was as strange as my day was going to get, but when we were ushered inside and presented to my very relieved father, we were informed that while the Third Order had not attacked the capital, there had been an attempt on cousin Addmaleta's life that morning, which Katjia's brother stopped. Three more assassins have been uncovered since. Making matters worse, Redgenold isn't even here. If I ever needed more proof that Veena's using him for something, there it is: Redge not turning up for dinner.

Needless to say, they took our warnings very seriously. Which is to say, everyone was so wrapped up in this whole assassination business, that they haven't heard a word Katjia or myself has said. There's an army of pirates coming for us, a double agent trying to steal our secret documents, and some mysterious replacement king in the shadows, but nobody cares. I'd have at least thought that my family would want to hear how I escaped and returned, but no... they probably didn't miss me.

Katjia says that they are relieved, and that they'll be dying to hear what has befallen me just as soon as they've made sure that there's no one in the palace still trying to kill us, but I don't believe her. This is just how little they care. And here I was, thinking they'd be worried sick about me. Well, maybe not all of them, but I thought at least Mayzin would have been in hysterics that I disappeared, but she's gone to Aunty Ettalara's house to plan Pippy's coming out. Katjia says that if I pitied myself less, things would be better. *Her* family was happy to have her back.

* * *

Kanara

The four nobles fixed him with steady gazes. It was somehow more excruciating than the thought of being shot by the erstwhile assassin. Kanara tried to stand up straight under their scrutiny. No need to put himself in a worse position than he already was.

Bernard explained in clipped tones everything that he had witnessed, and Kanara had the sense that he knew the royal family quite well.

"What is your name, tribesman?" the queen asked, when her butler had finished his tale.

"Kanara," he stated, his voice sounding hollow in his own ears.

"And you attempted to halt this assassin?"

"I saw him in the courtyard, your highness. I did not like the way he moved. He was dressed like a servant, so I did not think I would be looked upon kindly for screaming at him there and then, but I followed him inside, in case he was up to some mischief."

"And he went directly to Addmaleta's room?" the King inquired.

"I do not know the inside of this place well enough to say if the route was direct, but if you mean that he made no stops along the way, you would be correct."

"And when it became clear that he was hostile, you set upon him?" the captain of the guard asked, twirling the end of his mustache.

"I threw myself upon him from behind as he took aim," Kanara stated, trying

160

to keep the quaver from his voice.

"Then what happened?"

"I made sure that he was incapacitated, then ran to the princess to see if she was injured. She was not shot, but she collapsed momentarily from shock."

"I bet she said that was my fault," the queen said, glancing at her daughter ruefully.

"She did, your highness."

"Well, perhaps I should have let you train with the guards when you asked. I shouldn't have kidded myself into thinking that this place is always completely safe. Even here, it is best to have fighting skills. That being said, I hope you have learned that combat is neither exciting nor fun, and certainly nothing to be sought after, Addmaleta."

The princess, who had been standing resolutely beside Bernard, nodded sullenly.

"I do understand, mother."

"And the same goes for handsome tribesman. No offense to you, Kanara, you behaved most admirably, but sometimes my offspring forgets her manners."

"Why does everyone suddenly think I'm handsome? I look precisely as I did this morning. I've stopped an assassin, not gained a new face."

"Ah," said the captain of the guard, seeming amused by his insolence, "I think you will find that in the eyes of a young woman, those are one and the same thing."

The king cast his wife a look, and said, "Dear, may I remind you that you are not young?"

"No, you may not," she said. Kanara thought he saw a ghost of a smile flit across the king's lips.

"Be that as it may," the queen's lady took up the thread, "it seems that you have done us a great service. You don't need to cower before us like a criminal in need of punishment. You've done as well as anyone could and saved the princess's life. I, for one, am curious as to how this man evaded detection by all of the guards—every servant is thoroughly vetted. A stranger should have been apprehended at once."

There was still a slight Haputian drawl creeping in around the edges of her speech. Once again, Kanara sensed something rough and dangerous that wasn't buried quite so deep as it should have been. He tried to relax a little. It was clear that no one was angry with *him.*

"However he did it, we should be grateful that he wasn't expecting a family of nomads camped the the courtyard," the king said, looking at his daughter with barely veiled concern.

Redgenold nodded thoughtfully. "We will need to make sure that there aren't any more hidden killers in our midst. Addmaleta's cries for help will have ensured that all of the guards are alerted, but I should tell them to be on the lookout for people dressed as servants. Any suspicious activity and we will have them detained and questioned."

The king nodded. "Go, see to it. Your wife can guard us both for now."

The captain of the guard had hardly been gone for a minute, however, before he burst back into the room at top speed. Bernard, who had been comforting the princess, started so badly that he nearly fell over.

"The guards have already apprehended another man," Redgenold panted, "but that's not important. Marley and the nomad girl have returned, and they've brought a dragon with them!"

* * *

Katjia

Returning to the palace on dragonback had been one of the most terrifying experiences of Katjia's short life. It had given her a new appreciation for Marley's surprising bravery. She hadn't been able to see it as such for a long time, but there wasn't another word for someone willing to climb aboard a giant, purple, fire-breathing monster just to see his family again. Not only had he fearlessly clung to the dragon's back, he had gained the strength to look over the beasts heaving sides to the ground below before the trip was over. She was still amazed that the same boy who had screamed in terror at the mere thought of following the great four-toed tracks was now explaining why he had christened the she-dragon Eldrid.

"It means 'beautiful fire,'" he said.

They were sitting in his room, waiting for his father to return and tell them that it was safe to leave.

Veena must have had some way of communicating with the capital even faster than pigeon mail, for there had already been an attack within the palace itself before they had returned.

Fortunately, Kanara had been able to stop the would-be assassin, but the fact that killers had somehow infiltrated the staff without anyone noticing was terrifying. Katjia had been relieved to see her brother again, but their reunion had been short-lived, as Marley's father had called upon him to aid in the search for more hidden assassins. Everyone had agreed that it would be safest for her and the prince to stay out of the way.

* * *

She had been unsurprised to find that Marley's room was decorated entirely with ships. Even the curtains around his bed were made of dyed sail cloth.

They had both tried to sleep for an hour or so, but tired as they were, worry kept them both awake. Marley had scribbled in his diary for a little while, but eventually they had both taken to pacing. Their conversations were short and stilted.

Finally, he said, "It can't have been Veena. There's just no way she could have gotten a message to the palace that quickly. In fact, this whole event reeks of my brother Redgenold."

Katjia nodded. She didn't know Marley's brothers, but she agreed that Veena couldn't have been responsible for these attacks, not when she was already planning to send in the Third Order.

"Why, though," she asked, "why attempt assassination, in the middle of the palace, where you know there's hardly a chance of it working, even if you do have servants working for you."

"Probably to throw everyone off the scent. If Redge and Veena are working together to plan a coup, it would have been most effective if everyone was looking someplace else when the pirates got here."

"But do you really think it will work? Even assuming we never got off of The Tooth to warn anyone, I don't see such a small force of pirates being able to take over the capital. Veena never told us her whole plan, there must be some facet of it that we're missing."

Marley shook his head. "We already know who all the major players are, given the conversation I overheard. She made a deal with Redge to supply him with military supports, which must mean that he is planning some kind of insurrection. Unless..." he trailed off, looking out the window.

"Unless this whole thing is a distraction! Why didn't I see it before?" Katjia understood in an instant.

"There is no way that Veena would want Redge to be king! This attack must be intended to fail, which means that she's deceived him, along with everyone else. What could she gain from simply causing chaos?"

"Any number of things. If it were me, I want to try to get inside the keep and steal as many documents as possible. If you know that force is going to fail, blackmail could still work. Dart is usually on top of the palace, guarding the main tower, but with him gone—" He didn't need to finish.

"So she must have someone else already picked out to rule Laitmea. Somebody devious and smart, who will know what to do with all of your family's secrets."

"Exactly, and I don't have the first idea of how to prevent it. It would be hard enough to get anyone to take me seriously just saying that Redge is a threat. I'll never be able to get my father to move quickly enough. We might as well still be trapped on the tooth."

"Not necessarily. What would happen if we stole the documents first? There's no dragon guarding them now. He's off chasing Eldrid, trying to make baby dragons. We could empty out the keep and make a run for it before the Third Order gets here."

"Then what? They'd still attack the palace, and everyone would be in danger. Even if it's meant to fail, the battle with the pirates could still result in someone's death. Besides, people will think that my brother orchestrated the whole thing. Unless Veena is caught trying to steal the documents herself, no one will suspect her of anything, and she'll be free to try again. Redge will probably be hanged for treason when the plot wasn't his idea. I know he was complicit, but he doesn't deserve that!"

Katjia frowned, and started pacing again.

"What if we got there first—if the pirates knew that the documents had been removed?"

"Then they would come after us," said Marley.

"That would keep the attackers away from both of our families, and probably expose Veena's role in the plot. I don't see her leaving our capture up to somebody else. And it would also force Redge to come out of wherever he's hiding. If he's anything like you, he's not got the skills to survive on his own for that long—no offense to you, of course. If the promised soldiers don't come to start the attack, he's done for," Katjia stated. "So all around, it seems like the best way of foiling the pirates' plot. The only problem is, it would mean putting ourselves in even more danger. I'm not sure I relish the thought of running through the countryside with a pack of pirates chasing after us."

"I don't mind," said Marley, "I've gotten used to being scared out of my wits. If nobody around here is going to take my warnings seriously—and who can blame them with all these hidden assassins showing up—I've got to take matters into my own hands. Besides, we don't have to go on foot. We can take your horse."

"My horse is lost in the woods."

"Then what's that?" he asked, pointing out the window to the row of horses tied in the courtyard.

"...My horse. Isn't she clever? Well, that's settled. Where are we taking the documents? We'll need a safe-house of some kind, assuming the pirates don't catch us. Even if your parents take action the minute they realize what the real danger is, we could still spend days trying to evade them."

"Aunty Ettalara's house," Marley said without pause. "That's where Mayzin is, along with all the other reasonable people who'll actually listen to me and know that Veena is the real threat, not Redge and his fake coup. It's far enough away that we can lose the pirates in the countryside before arriving, and well defended. You'd have to be insane to attack the estate directly."

"That settles it. We'll wait to depart until we can be sure that the Third Order is close enough that someone will see us leave and follow us. I'll get the horse ready, and then we can storm the keep."

Marley agreed, already re-packing his bag. "Once you have Petrushka saddled, can you get us some more cheese? I have a felling we're going to need it."

* * *

Kanara

The relief Kanara felt upon seeing his sister again was a force beyond words. A knot in his chest he had not even realized he was carrying had eased the moment Redgenold announced her safe return.

Soon enough, she was hugging him tightly around the middle. Her clothes were dirty and crusted with salt from the sea, her staff was missing, and her pack was broken and mostly depleted, but she was *safe*. Marley was likewise battered but unharmed.

Kanara heard only garbled fragments of Katjia's explanation for her disappearance, caught up as he was in the joy of her return. What he did make out was enough to put him into a truly titanic rage. It was the first time anyone had mentioned a girl called Veena in his presence, but he decided at once that he wished to see her dead.

The only thing stopping him from running out to find and destroy his sister's would-be attackers was the remaining threat of actual attackers within the palace itself. The servant he had incapacitated had been identified as a recent hire who had previously worked on the estate of the king's chamberlain. This explained how he had been able to slip by unnoticed. It was assumed that he had been properly vetted by his previous employer. It did not, however, remove the possibility of more hidden assassins.

It seemed that the only servant the royal family completely trusted was Bernard, for he had been one of the first men they hired after the death of

Darin the Terrible, nearly twenty years ago.

Thus, Kanara, though loath to leave Katjia so soon after being reunited, was more than willing to be pressed into service hunting through the palace for more armed men. *Better,* he thought, *that I see to it myself. I don't think I trust another soul with my sister's well being, even Bernard.*

* * *

Jessimin

In Jessimin's opinion, the only saving grace of their trip to Aunt Ettalara's house was the fact that she didn't have to share a room with cousin Evayah. Their last visit had been with the whole family, and the great house had been so full that she had been forced to sleep on a small cot. The cot hadn't been all that uncomfortable, but being stuck with a miniature of Ettalara had been. Jessimin had always prided herself on having excellent manners, pleasant conversational abilities, and a good sense of style. Such things were not enough for Evayah.

In this household, it didn't matter if you had the cleanest hands at the table; the fact that those hands had voluntarily touched tree bark earlier in the day made them despicable. As much as she knew that it was necessary, Jessimin had hated every minute of this trip so far.

Today, her cousins were out visiting a friend, and Jessimin was relieved to find that she had the entire lower level of the house to herself. Her first act was to find the most salacious romance novel in the library, and ensconce herself in a doily-covered armchair to read. Whatever was coming would come, and she didn't feel like wasting her time worrying about things that were out of her control. She rang for the cook and had a glass of lemonade brought to her, which she knew her aunt would disapprove of. She drank it all without spilling a drop and reveled in the thought that she had held a full glass over the carpet.

Around midday, there was a knock at the front door, and a clatter as the butler hurried to answer it. Jessimin set down her book, intrigued. It was likely nothing, but still worth investigating. She made her way down the hall just as the door closed behind a messenger boy. The butler had three letters on his silver tray.

"Anything for me?" Jessimin asked, peering at the stack.

"All post is to be directed to the lady of the house, princess."

"Even if it's not hers? That seems a little odd."

"Forgive me, princess. I do not make the rules, I simply abide by them."

"But that looks like Kessie's handwriting. She won't have written to Aunt Ettalara," Jessimin made a grab for the letter, and the butler was so stunned that she was able to take the whole lot. She glanced at the other two, which were indeed addressed to Ettalara and discarded them back on the tray, taking Kestly's letter back to the library. The butler gave an indignant huff, before starting up the stairs to deliver the other letters to his Lady's room.

Jessimin knew that she should get Pippy and Mayzin from upstairs before opening the letter, but it was too hard to wait. Her sisters didn't hate every day they spent here. They would be fine without news for a few more minutes.

* * *

Dear Jessi, Mayzin, and Pipps.

I probably should have asked the three of you why you wanted me to watch our brother. Then again, I should have known that you wouldn't have gone through the trouble of getting our mail out of the furnace for entertainment. More's the pity.

He's up to something for sure. Burned a dozen more letters—my guess is from a lady. I couldn't read any of them, but the envelopes smelled like flowers and the wax seals were dyed purple. At first, I thought you were being overly paranoid and he just has a girl stashed somewhere, but then I saw him hiding a gun in his desk.

Then, last night (two nights ago by the time this reaches you) he left with the gun in his hand. I followed him as far as the aspen copse on the other side of the river, but there I lost his trail. Not a soul has seen him since, but given that he was carrying a pack and several other weapons, I'd say he plans to be gone for a while. I don't know who he might meet in the woods. There's not much in the way of scum that he couldn't invite into a tavern.

If I didn't know better, I'd say he's about to attack someone.

Anyway, I hope you're not going to reveal anything... even if I failed in one regard. I trust you three to make the right decision.

Kestly

∗ ∗ ∗

Katjia

The entrance to the highest tower of the palace—affectionately known as The Keep by those who lived there, though it bore no resemblance to the keeps of traditional Haputian castles for which it was named—was unmanned when Marley and Katjia reached it.

Katjia supposed that it probably would have been pointless. If anyone found a way past the great green dragon, the guards at the gate, and every servant wandering the halls, one more pair of eyes wasn't going to prevent them from taking everything inside. Still, it was eerie to haul open the heavy black walnut door without another soul around.

They stepped inside. Unlike the other wings of the palace, which were divided into five floors, the keep was one massive column, rising up an additional two stories behind the throne room with only a spiral staircase to break its sheer walls.

"I feel like I'm standing inside a giant drum," Katjia said, staring up at the distant ceiling. There was a ring of small windows between the top two turns of the stairs, which provided scant illumination. The light was only enough to reveal faint glints and gleams of the treasures kept there.

Shadows clung to everything, muting colors and hiding details. She stepped further into the chamber and saw that the walls were lined with thousands of artifacts. Armor hung on hooks, many feet above their heads. A few spans past the softly glittering breastplates, she saw racks of scrolls, likely older than her grandfather's grandfather.

There were gems, of course, as she had know there would be, rubies and sapphires and golden bracelets, but the objects that held her attention were less flashy. Hunting horns and horse tack, books and bowstrings, and even a small harp were stored neatly on the floor. The air was dry, but not dusty, ideal for preserving priceless artifacts.

Marley was already moving up the spiral staircase by the time she had finished admiring his family's wealth, both of riches and knowledge.

"The newest things are kept closest to the ground. More likely that somebody will need them. Things from my mother's childhood are going to be a few floors up," he said, beckoning to her. "Probably more floors up than she would be entirely comfortable with, I think," he added.

Katjia stuck close to the wall as she ascended. The drop was no greater than the cliffs around Pirate's Cove, but it still made her uncomfortable.

"So the things at the top are from the distant past? Valuables and heirlooms and such?"

"Yes and no. There are some really lovely crowns from the last millennium, and some original copies of scholarly writings, but up at the very top, where the light comes in, is where my aunty likes to store paintings of past monarchs she considers ugly."

"Won't that damage the canvas?"

"Not as much as leaving them out would have. There was one bloke who my mother kept punching whenever she walked by. Said he reminded her of the orphanage headmistress."

"That is unfortunate."

Now that they were higher up, she could indeed see a ring of portraits just beneath the windows. What she could make out made her sure that she didn't want to get any closer.

"It's probably a good thing that some Haputian blood got mixed into the royal family," Marley noted, following her gaze.

As he looked back at her, his green eyes went wide, and he cocked his head to the side. "You're beautiful."

Katjia was sure that if her skin were any paler, she would have blushed scarlet. It was so abrupt. It sounded as if he had just noticed that she existed, yet he commented as if it was the most natural thing in the world. Given how infrequently the prince looked at people, she supposed that to him, it was.

"No one has ever said that to me before," she said, smiling slightly.

"Really?" He was rummaging in an alcove of the step above him now, his back to her. "I suppose nobody wants to state the obvious."

If it were anyone else speaking to her, Katjia would have wondered if she were being insulted, but having been kept in such close confinement with Marley for so long, she knew that he would never have meant it as such.

"No, it's typically something said by people who have very serious intentions." She wondered if she should elaborate. "Between my father's death and leaving for Laitmea, I've never been close enough with a man my own age for such things to be appropriate. I suppose had I stayed in the desert, and spent more time with families not my own, I would have heard it a dozen times by now."

"Do you wish you had stayed?" he asked, passing her a stack of letters, bound with a satin ribbon.

"No, Prince Marley. I liked hearing it from you."

"Then I shall tell you every day, until we are both so old that we forget." He straightened up, holding several small books and another stack of papers.

"Your intentions are *that* serious?"

"They are," he said, and started back down the stairs. "We have all of the important evidence, as far as I can tell. Time to wait for our pursuers."

"Wait," she shrieked, running after him, all fear of heights forgotten. She caught him at the bottom of the stairs and kissed him. For a moment, books and papers were forgotten, and the world was perfect.

"They'll say we're too young," she whispered, drawing away. "They'll say it's not right for a prince and a peasant..."

He raised an eyebrow. "They'll say nothing of the sort. Everyone will count it a small miracle that I found a girl willing to kiss me. Including me."

"Then let's go wait for the pirates," Katjia said, heading for the door.

* * *

174

Veena

I had hoped that the conclusion to this account would be written in the next few hours, but our arrival at Lyrah did not go as planned.

Carsten and I rode with our men back through the dust lands, the forest, and the Laitmean countryside to meet Redgenold just outside the city limits. We located our leader without much difficulty, though it was a chore keeping such a large host undetected in such a populated area.

I then went ahead towards the city gate, but just before I reached the bridge, I saw a lone horse with two riders, cantering down the road. To my horror, I saw that Marley and Katjia had somehow managed to beat us to our target. What was more, I saw in Katjia's hands a stack of papers that could only be the letters and other documents that we were after. I cursed my speeches about our order's impending good fortune. I must have let something slip that allowed the prince to guess a little too much of our plan.

I racked my brain as I returned to tell Carsten and Redgenold to ready the men for a chase, but I couldn't think what I had said that would let them glean what we were after. Perhaps Marley simply knows his brother a little too well. What I don't understand is how they managed to get off The Tooth. There was no vessel they could have sailed across in, and even if they had constructed a raft, they would have washed ashore miles and miles from civilization with no means of transportation. I can't believe that they would have walked the distance quicker than we have ridden. It should have taken them months to return, not hours. And they should not have returned at all.

I then realized that Redgenold was going to be liability. I couldn't just explain to him that his coup was never the real point of the plot, or that I had already organized to have his forces crushed by a more suitable candidate. I had to leave him with a small number of the Third Order, after telling him that somebody had spotted us, and that we needed to track the unnamed party down before they jeopardized our plan. It only worked because he is quite a fool. I only hope that his idiocy keeps him in position for however long it takes. We've been tracking Marley and Katjia all night and most of the morning, but they've been keeping just ahead of us. If we don't recapture them soon, the whole plan may be in jeopardy.

I will expound further upon this miserable turn of events soon.

* * *

Kanara

Kanara had spent the evening after the assassination attempt in a secure room on the first floor of the palace. Now, he paced the halls, wondering what to do next. Redgenold the elder had moved his entire family in from the courtyard, lest they become targets as well. There had been ten servants found with weapons of various sorts, and half a dozen more who had been taking turns in the Lord Captain of the Guard's office for questioning.

So far, the only things that the investigation had turned up were a few packets of lead shot, and the fact that almost all of the servants-turned-killers had once worked for the Chamberlain Donis and his wife Ettalara. The rest of the staff were tiptoeing around in varying degrees of shock.

Kanara tapped a maid on the shoulder as she passed, and asked "Excuse me miss, but where is my sister staying? I need to consult with her."

Katjia would know what to do. She always had the confidence to come up with a course of action, and Kanara could do with a dose of that confidence now. Stopping the gunman had rattled him more than he had initially suspected.

"The girl Katjia? She is with Prince Marley."

Kanara ground his teeth. It was as plain as the nose on his face that the two of them were falling in love. His sister could do far worse than a prince, even if he wasn't likely to be king. Still, they were both young, and liable to do something foolish. Come to think of it, their relationship thus far had been built on one foolish decision after another.

He went to the prince's room, but found it empty. He glanced at the array of ship models, and spotted a piece of paper on the bedspread. He picked it up and squinted at the sloppy writing on it. It had been years since he had needed to read anything, and it took him a few minutes to work out the cramped script.

Dear Reader,

If anyone finds this, please know that Katjia and I are fine. We have taken several papers with us, and are heading to a safe location. Should the pirates overrun the palace, they won't find what they are looking for. Hopefully, they will have already followed us and now be hopelessly lost in the hills. Hope this letter finds whoever is reading it well, unless it's Veena. We told Eldrid to eat her if she dares to set foot in the keep.

Sincerely, Prince Marley Michaell Frederick of Laitmea.

The note was written on the back of a piece of waxed paper, and smelled faintly of cheese. Kanara heaved a sigh, swore at the cheese paper, and went to find the Captain of the Guard.

* * *

ELDRID & DART

Marley

Shortly after my last entry, Katjia and I realized that the pirates' impending attack was doomed to fail. We could only conclude that it was meant as a distraction from whatever Veena's real plans were, so we did the only logical thing.

We broke into the Keep, and stole any valuable documents that Veena could possibly want. Then we took Petrushka just outside of the city to wait. We were out almost the whole night before we saw the telltale signs of a small army approaching. We made sure that we were fully visible to the lead pirates, papers and all, and then set off at a breakneck pace.

For the first few miles, we could even hear the pirates shouting. Our guess had been correct; they weren't out to take over the capital like Redge thinks they are. They're trying to start a smear campaign against my parents and the queen with the information from their old notebooks.

Now, we've drawn far enough ahead that we can take short breaks. We don't want them to lose our trail until they're well away from our families in the capital, so for now, traveling has been easy. We're going to go to Aunty Ettalara's house, as it is far from the capital, defensible, and that is where Mayzin is.

I still can't believe that she left to plan a party while I was kidnapped by pirates. Katjia said that I'm overreacting. Maybe Mayzin caught on to Redge's plans and went to seek advice from the least insane adult in our family?

Anyway, I suppose that it's only right to mention that while we were in the Keep, Katjia and I kissed. I still feel awful that I got us stranded on The Tooth, but when I tried to tell her that it was my fault last night, she wouldn't listen and just kissed me again and said that all was forgiven. I thought she would be furious that I left without telling her that the door was open, but she's not.

Either I don't understand her as well as I think I do, or she's in love with me. I never thought any girl would be, given that everyone at home looks at me like I'm crazy every time I open my mouth. But Katjia's not just any girl; she's pretty and funny, and very good and knocking people unconscious with her staff. More than could be said for me, at any rate. She's not bad to kiss, either.

* * *

Katjia

Katjia knew that Petrushka would have been able to cover the distance to Lady Ettalara's home far quicker than any of the pirates' animals, but the goal was not to outstrip them completely. She had led the horse at a far more moderate pace than she had during the ride after the diplomats to teasing their pursuers. She had been able to show Marley how to ride competently and had allowed short breaks for food and sleep.

Now, with the final leg of their journey upon them, she pushed Petrushka to a breakneck speed. Marley was behind her, arms wrapped firmly around her waist. Their last glimpse of the Third Order had been that morning and she doubted they would see them again. She wondered if enough time had passed for those still at the palace to have figured out the plot. She hoped that the younger Redgenold had been apprehended. She hoped that Veena could be stopped.

Mostly, she hoped that her brother wouldn't be too angry with her for running away again. She knew that he didn't deserve such a pain for a sister; he would be worried sick and rightly so. She resolved that when next they met, she and Kanara would sit down and have a long talk about Gynn. They needed to. Then, if there was time, she would bring up the topic of Marley. Even thinking about that made her go hot all over.

The prince was so very different from everyone else she knew, but in her heart, she felt that it was not such a bad thing. He was more generous and quicker to forgive than he had a right to be. He was honest to a fault. If he said hurtful things, it was never because he wanted to, but because he didn't think that they were hurtful. If he had half as much passion for her as he had for ships, they would be in love with each other until the sun burned itself into darkness. He was a prince. Surely, her brother couldn't object to a *prince.*

If Marley was troubled by any of these thoughts, he didn't show it. He spoke rarely, preferring to focus on maintaining his hold on her and the horse, only occasionally giving her directions. Katjia had been guiding them steadily eastward, but she could not bring them to an estate she had never seen before. The closer they came, the more heavily she had to rely on Marley's recollection. She hoped that his sense of direction was as good as his sense of ship building. If it wasn't, they were in deep trouble.

At last, they crested a small hill, and saw the house in the distance. It was an impressive building, with graceful stone columns and hundreds of glittering glazed windows. Marley had described it to her quite well, but the sheer size of it still took Katjia aback. It was almost as big as the palace, with twice the amount of garden. There was even an ornamental lake, with a black swan floating upon its surface. There were a dozen outbuildings scattered around, as well as an apple orchard, and miles of manicured gravel paths. All of the wealth she had seen in the capital paled in comparison to this.

So dazed by her surroundings, Katjia nearly let Petrushka crash into a boulder half concealed under the moss. She slowed to a canter and then to a stop, before they reached the great front entryway.

"What now?" she asked, wondering how many varieties of roses was too many.

"Now, we knock on the door and hope it's not cousin Donis who answers. He's an insufferable fool, with far too much good breeding for my taste."

"And where shall Petrushka go?"

"In the stable with the other horses. She can teach them a thing or two."

Katjia patted her steed, nodding. "She could indeed."

* * *

Jessimin

Mayzin and Pippy had been suitably shocked by Kestly's letter when Jessimin had at last made it upstairs. What disturbed Jessimin more than her brother's disappearance, however, was the way the butler had treated a letter clearly addressed to her.

She still couldn't shake the feeling that something was wrong. It had settled in her chest like a cough, and every time she looked at a servant or her Aunt, Jessimin could feel it flare to life again. She tried to bring this up to her sisters, but they were too busy discussing what Redge could possibly be doing. They did not, however, bring up the contents of the letter to Ettalara at dinner, or the next day.

If anyone besides the butler was angry that Jessimin had snatched her post without permission, they didn't show it, but she did notice that Evayah was suddenly much more interested in spending time with her. Jessimin was sure that the pint-sized noblewoman was acting on her mother's orders, but why Ettalara wanted to inspect every incoming letter was a mystery to her.

Hours crept by unnoticed in the enormous house, and Jessimin's feelings of unease only grew. Her cousin Donis was nowhere to be found, not that she much wanted to talk to him, and her Uncle was holed up in his study for most of the day with the door barred.

Though their trip was supposed to be a mission to prevent Redge from taking the throne by force, everything was now moving so slowly that Jessimin

184

felt more like a prisoner than anything else. She wondered if Marley was all right, and if he or Katjia would ever return. She read every romance novel the library had to offer, and then read a few she slipped from Evayah's room, though they weren't nearly as good, and her cousin didn't even notice that they were missing.

At some point, Mayzin had grown so bored that she actually did begin to plan Pippy's coming out party. Pippy made half-hearted attempts to help her, then gave up and started reading the more interesting novels that Jessimin had finished. At least once a day, one of the girls would bring up the reason for their stay with their aunt, but the answer was always the same. She was doing what she could, letters were being sent, but they needed to be patient. This was the safest place for them.

Within a few days, Jessimin suspected that it soon wouldn't be a safe place for anyone else. If nothing happened, she was going to go crazy and kill them all.

As if her thoughts had been some kind of magic, she heard a knock at the door an instant later.

"I'll get it," she cried, jumping up at once. It might be the butler's job, but Jessimin was closer, and nothing was going to stop her from opening the door herself. It wasn't ladylike or proper, but it was what she wanted to do.

"You'll go upstairs at once!" said Ettalara, appearing by the door as if by magic. Jessimin was tempted to swear.

"It is not ladylike or proper for a princess to open the front door. I'll get the butler and do it the right way, while you go to your room and review your etiquette."

Jessimin knew better than to fight her aunt.

"It's not even my room," she hissed under her breath as she mounted the stairs, "and you're not even a blood relative. I don't know why I call you aunty. Mother knew best when she said she'd feed you to a dragon."

She did not go to the guest room she was supposed to be in, but dashed to the nearest window instead. There, to her utter amazement, she could see Marley and the nomad girl Katjia. She watched Ettalara let them in, then ran down the hall to tell Pippy and Mayzin. Marley was alive and well, and Aunt

Ettalara was up to something. The butler hadn't been the one to answer the door.

* * *

Marley

We've lost the pirates and made it safely to Aunty Ettalara's estate. Uncle Donis is one of Uncle Dowlin's advisors, so they're quite well-off. Their house is a tad stuffy for my taste, and their son Donis III is an insufferable prick, but at least we're not being chased through the countryside anymore.

Aunty Ettalara greeted us at the door and gave us scones and lemonade, then left us in the parlor. She said that she had just received an urgent letter that needed to be tended to immediately, and that she'd listen to our woes when she got back. I don't know, though, something seems off.

Mayzin joined us a little later, along with Jessimin and Pippy, and said that Ettalara is going to be a little longer than expected. I had hoped that she would take our warnings seriously, but she hasn't even heard them yet.

At least my fears about Mayzin were proved wrong. She had indeed worked out that Redge was conspiring with Veena to overthrow the king and queen. She's been here long enough to bring it up to Aunty, and she said that her urgent letter is probably in regards to the Redge problem. She was also suitably shocked that we had evaded and tricked the pirates as we had. I suppose that there's no harm in saying that, now that we're here safely.

We only moved mother's diary up a few floors in the keep, in case the pirates didn't take the bait. Veena would have had a much harder time finding what she wanted, at least. But they did follow us, even though the papers we were holding were actually this diary and all last month's dinner menus. Even if they send someone into the palace undercover, at least a dozen servants will tell them that they saw us leave the keep just hours before the chase started. It was mostly Katjia's idea. One more reason for me to love her. We gave the menus to Pippy for safekeeping.

* * *

We've just received word from Kestly; Pippy had to snatch the letter from the butler before he took all the mail to Ettalara, and it's a good thing she did.

Our sister wrote to say that Katjia and myself had briefly returned to the palace, and that she now believed that we were on our way to the Chamberlain's estate.

Well, we beat the letter here, but Kestly made a good guess. She said that Kanara had found our note. I had almost hoped it would be Veena, if only so Eldrid could eat her. We told the dragon that pirates taste like cheese.

Then Kestly went on to say that she informed the rest of father's guards that Redgenold was probably behind the attempted assassinations, and that he was hiding in the woods, waiting for the pirates to begin his attack. The guards were able to track him down, and lock him up, pending formal punishment.

Our note to Kanara, of course explained the rest. But the shocking news was something else all together. According to Kestly, all of the would be assassins were real servants. They were people who used to work for Ettalara, who took jobs at the palace a few years ago. We had never bothered to look into their pasts, because we assumed that the king's own advisor wouldn't send us bad servants. But this raises a whole host of new questions.

Is Ettalara somehow behind some of this violence? I can't think that she would want Katjia and me kidnapped, or Mer's diplomat murdered in the forest, or Addmaleta shot, but still, it's a little fishy. I think Veena might have even more tricks up her sleeve than we originally thought.

Anyway, it's a good thing that our aunt didn't have a chance to read the letter, because Kessie told us that mother and father, and maybe even the king and queen, will be coming out here in just a day or two to confront Donis and Ettalara about the servants personally, and also to ask how the pirates even knew that the diaries and letters they're after existed in the first place. The Keep holds many things, but most of them are secrets. Somebody had to tell Veena that they were in there, and it certainly wasn't me.

* * *

Katjia

Katjia closed the stable door, hoping that Petrushka would be alright. The Laitmean horses were bigger than her and looked like they might bite. She had picketed her horse along a fence when they first arrived, but this had greatly upset the gardener, so she had agreed to move Petrushka to the stable. She had never been in a stable before, and the only other horses she had known were from her own family.

Still, it was probably safer than being outside, and it was certainly safer than the trek she had made back through the forest and countryside all on her own. Katjia was still amazed that the animal had managed to find her way back to Kanara without any assistance. She wondered how terrified Kanara had been to see her riderless, and resolved to apologize to her brother the next time she saw him.

The night before, they had received word that Marley's parents were on their way to sort everything out. Cheery as Kestly's letter had been, Katjia doubted anyone's ability to sort *everything* out. She could just now see carriages in the distance, which must have been them. She wondered at the speed they must have traveled at. Even with the best boats, making such good time was extraordinary. Kestly's letter, sent by pigeon, had barely beaten them.

Whatever Marley might say about his parents not caring about him, it was clear to her that only a mother's love could drive someone to such lengths.

In a family with eight children, she could see that the prince sometimes felt overlooked, but here was concrete proof that he was not.

Katjia knew that she should probably make herself scarce while the royal family was arriving and unpacking. They didn't need one more person in the way, and if things turned sour, as she knew they might, she didn't want to witness it. She turned away from the house, intending to take a stroll through the vast gardens.

There, not ten paces down the path, she saw Veena. The road had not been kind to the pirate; her blond hair was disheveled, her cloak full of burrs, and her dress torn. Katjia at once regretted leading their pursuers through so many brambles and thickets. At the time, it had seemed like a good idea, but now Veena was fuming angry and carrying a knife. She leveled the blade at Katjia's chest, and rasped, "Where are they?"

Katjia didn't have to ask what she meant. "Inside. But you'll be caught the moment you set foot in there. The king and queen have brought all of their guards and they know what you intend to do. Most of it, at least."

"Don't try to talk your way out of this, nomad. I'll have you flayed alive and spit-roasted when this is all done. I've got Carsten positioning a thousand men around this estate, and I don't care who I have to kill to make this work."

Katjia didn't doubt her. She only wished that she hadn't left her new tree-branch staff tied up with Petrushka's saddle bags.

"Shall we go in, then?" she asked, supposing that the best policy was to keep the mad woman happy.

"After you, my dear," Veena said, gesturing with her knife.

* * *

191

Jessimin

The last few days had been overwhelming, to say the least, and Jessimin wanted nothing more than to jump into her mother's arms like a small child and beg to be taken home.

Marley's safe arrival had not been celebrated so much as shoved under the rug and forgotten about. Jessimin had been intrigued to meet the nomad girl and hear their stories, but her aunt had hushed any attempts at dinner conversation. Uncle Dowlin had seemed genuinely pleased to see the pair, but that had been the end of it.

Then, after dinner, a second letter from Kestly had arrived, informing them that Redgenold had been captured and their parents would shortly be coming to see them. Jessimin doubted that anyone had ever felt such instantaneous relief. If there was a problem that Quipeneay couldn't fix, she hadn't met it yet.

But it still wasn't clear whether there was a problem or not. Perhaps Ettalara and Donis were just being themselves, and it was all in her head. Perhaps the only reason her aunt wanted all the mail for herself was to get the responses to her calls for help as quickly as possible. Jessimin hadn't been able to sleep that night, wandering as she was in a forest of perhapses. Now, her parents were here, and all was right with the world.

The king and queen were with them, looking as impressive as always, and Jessimin had the distinct impression that they had dressed especially to be intimidating. The king was in his ceremonial military garb, the queen in a tight fitted dark blue gown with diamond accents. Why they had dressed so was beyond her. This was their finest, not their traveling clothes.

Father was in the stripped-down, everyday version of Dowlin's gear, complete with a sword and gun. Mother was in red, as she always was, with no adornment and no hint of softness. Her hair was kept cropped in army style, her skirts slit for mobility. If it wasn't mother, Jessimin would have been very frightened. Quipeneay was wearing a look on her face that could have killed. It was a look that had preceded very many killings in the past.

Marley and her sisters were just behind her as she ran down the stairs to greet them. They had been sitting by the windows all day, hardly talking, passing Kestly's letter between them and waiting for the promised visitors. Evayah had tried to talk to them, but the four siblings had refused to tell her anything. Ettalara didn't need a chance to prepare for her own family.

Redgenold the elder immediately set down the queen's traveling bag and folded Marley and Mayzin in a bone-crushing hug. Pippy let out a small squeak and wrapped herself around the outside of the huddle. Jessimin watched them with a feeling of unreality, then turned to face her mother.

"Something's wrong," she whispered, making no move to join the exuberant greetings.

"I know," said Quip, fingering the hilt of a knife sticking out of her sleeve, "I'm here to fix it. You've done very well, coming here, blackmailing your sister. You don't have to worry about anything. I'll make it all right."

"You know about Kestly?"

"Everything? No. But enough. You're all my daughters, and it's foolish of you to forget it."

"Then did you know about Redgie? And Veena?"

"If I had been paying attention, I would have. But Mer's diplomat was successful as a distraction, if nothing else. We were all so concerned about what the government of Mer was going to do, so wrapped up in our peace treaties and machinations, that we weren't looking at the real show. I failed you in that regard. It shouldn't have taken Marley getting kidnapped and returning on a dragon to alert me to a problem with my own children. I hope you'll forgive me for that bit o' malarkey. Bungled it, I did."

Jessimin felt the corner of her mouth twitch up into a smile. He mother's accent never failed to slip out at the most inopportune times. "I think I can say we forgive you on behalf of all of us. It's not every day a diplomat storms out of the throne room in a rage. I'm just glad you're here now."

They shared a glace at Redgenold, who was tousling the twins' hair and making grandiose proclamations about declaring the day a holiday for the whole land.

Trilliapa and Dowlin had shouldered their own traveling bags and were trying to push past the mayhem.

"This isn't normal behavior for royalty, is it?" Jessimin asked, bemused.

"Not in the slightest. But the country prospers more than it ever did under proper leadership, so do us a favor and don't bring up etiquette. Speaking of which…"

Ettalara and Donis were coming down the hall, both looking almost as murderous as Quip.

"You should have told us you were coming!" Ettalara exclaimed.

"And give you a chance to throw us out?" snorted Quip, patting Jessimin on the head.

"Please," Donis interjected, "the hallway is hardly the place for receiving guests, announced or not. Let's have all the adults come through to the parlor. The butler can take the bags."

Just as suddenly as they had come, they were all gone. The parlor door clicked shut not a moment later, and three disgruntled princesses and one prince were left standing in the hall. Marley kicked the floor, wringing his hands. Pippy whistled through her teeth. Jessimin pressed her ear to the keyhole, but caught only muffled snatches of conversation. Her mother was telling someone about how Redgenold's planned attack seemed to be nothing but a diversion, she thought.

"I can't make out a thing," she whispered. Mayzin tapped her on the shoulder, and pointed up the stairs. Evayah was standing on the top step, rocking back and forth.

"Don't tell your mother we were eavesdropping!" Pippy hissed, throwing the young woman a rude gesture. Evayah teetered for a moment more, then descended the stairs.

"I don't like what's going on any more than you do," she said, biting her lip. "If you want to listen in, there's another door. It opens up behind a tapestry, so you can hear everything without being seen."

"I'll go, and report back," Mayzin volunteered, and followed their cousin. Marley whispered, "wait for me," and trotted after them, leaving Jessimin and Pippy alone.

Evayah returned a moment later. "There's not enough room for three," she said. "We'll have to make do with the keyhole."

Jessimin nodded and bent to listen once more. This time, she could make out the voices a little better. The adults must have seated themselves closer to the door. She listened with growing horror. She could only imagine what the twins must have been seeing.

* * *

The Lady

"Those documents were kept absolutely secret. Only someone within the royal family could have alerted the pirates in the first place,"

Dead silence followed Donis' statement, as everyone tried to grasp its enormous implications. Someone had betrayed Laitmea, but to what end?

"Don't say such things" Ettalara cried, "Surely there was some other way. None of us would dare betray the crown!"

Her knuckles were white. Clenching the folds of her skirt, she looked on the verge of tears.

"That is a heavy accusation," Dowlin admitted, eyes roving about the room, "but it does put you out of the spotlight when questions have to be asked,"

Donis bridled, glaring at his wife and the king in turn. "As if I would attempt to kill my own brother? Any interest I ever expressed in the throne was voided when I achieved an advisory position. Even if I still craved power, I would not kill my own flesh and blood to attain it. Unlike some." He cast Dowlin an disdainful look, "but it is becoming increasingly clear that foul play is afoot."

Trilliapa raised her eyebrows, regal incredulity one of her only convincingly royal expressions. "You must be accusing someone. If there is a rat in our midst, we need to have a reasonable assurance of cornering him, or her, else our accusations might only cause them to bolt."

Quip, legs thrown over the arm of a chair in a manner calculated to cause any true lady discomfort, gave a raucous snort. "Actually, Trill, the nincompoop knows what he's about, for once. If someone did betray the crown, every suspect is present and accounted for. Beyond you, the king, myself and my husband, Donis and Ettalara are the only ones who knew the whole content of the letters."

Redge smiled, a roguish devil-may-care look flashing across his face. The years had done nothing to diminish his looks. "Just like old times. Secret documents in the wrong hands, kingdoms about to collapse, assassinations planned, and the six of us in the thick of it."

Donis shot him a glare. "Well, if you think old times were good times, you're the only one. Maybe you planned this whole fiasco."

Redge maintained his smile, but there was a tightness to it now. "Well, we all knew you were taking a stab in the dark, but even considering that, you have bad aim. If I informed the pirates, or even egged on my son, I would be jeopardizing my position. Not to mention that I'd be plotting against my friend and king. Furthermore, if I wanted my son on the throne, why would I turn around and expose him? I am not a man who destroys family, friends, and good name for power, any more than you are!"

Donis did not argue, but nor did he have the good grace to look ashamed. He moved on the the next attack. "What of your lunatic wife then? She has ties to the pirates already, and we all know she finds peace and quiet boring. Perhaps she decided to cause a little mayhem just for kicks."

"I have ears, you know," Quip stated before her husband could martial a defense, "and I don't appreciate being called a lunatic."

"Accusing her is as foolish as accusing Redgenold," Trill cut in. "I highly doubt that my best friend of twenty-four years would orchestrate my death. Or endanger her children's futures, for that matter."

This time Ettalara came to Donis' defense, "You have ties to the pirates as well, you know. Fine thing to talk about loyalty and children, what says *you* didn't want out of the stuffy nobility life? Or your husband, for that matter. Faking your deaths is just the sort of romantic activity I would expect from monarchs with shady pasts."

"Well, we all know my dear brother is too in love with his throne to want out," Donis said, thoughtful now. "But perhaps he was regretting his hasty choice of spouse? And there's only about a thousand ways a war could help his waning luster in the public eye."

"If I cared for public opinion, having my wife killed wouldn't be high on my list of priorities. Even if I hated her, I wouldn't do it. Not have the humble orphan who rose to power by grit and determination alone standing by my side? I'd as soon hold court in my undergarments," Dowlin subsided into an embarrassed silence. The room, now ringed by flushed and angry faces, was quiet. The tick of a grandfather clock, the buzz of a single fly, and overwhelming silence pressed upon their ears.

Quip smirked, green eyes roving over each of them in turn, and as they did, her grin widened. A low, deranged chuckling emanated from her throat, slowly building until she was overcome by mirth, head tossed back and tears trickling into her hair.

Everyone, even Redge, stared at her, and she returned their looks with pure venom. The laughter seemed to go on forever, a disconcerting, gasping babble of noise. Then she hiccuped herself into a semblance of sanity, and said, "Fine thing for us to go on rambling and fighting and accusing each other, when we all know full well who the culprit is!"

Confusion. Half asked questions clashing with barely understandable accusations in a burst of noise. Quip was laughing again. "Who's the only one of us who doesn't stand to lose anything in this little game?" She asked and once again had the rapt attention of the group. "Who's the only one who could gain from the royal family's death, my son's mad rampage, war with the pirates?"

And now she was mad, dangerously mad, her eyes teary red and gleaming.

"Which one of us has been hoping for my disgrace and demise since they day I came to be called princess? Which one of us thinks that Trill and Dowlin oughtn't to rule? Which one of us has covered her tracks, so as to have no motive, no blame? Which one of us has plotted for months, years, maybe, to take back what is perceived as birthright, not for herself, but for her son? Does Donis know, or do you work alone?"

Ettalara had become as milk white as the fine china in her dining hall, with furious splotches of crimson rising on her cheeks, but her voice was deadly calm.

"How could Donis know? It was his father, Darin, who first ascended to the throne by treachery. When he was rightfully slain for his crimes, the throne ought not to have passed on to his son. Had my mother lived, it would have been *her* birthright. It is in *my* veins that the *true* royal blood flows, undiluted by treason or Haputian stock. For all his noble bearing, my husband has no more right to sit on the throne than his halfwit brother. My aim has only and ever been to give Laitmea its good and rightful king. *My son.*"

"So you admit to treason!" Quip snarled, half rising in her chair.

"Treason? I contacted the Third Order, sending letters under a false name. I told them of the younger Redgenold's disposition and suggested that he would be an excellent rally point for an uprising,"

"Which would have led to assassination!"

"Which would have led to nothing of the sort. It merely would have weakened both the Third Order and the Laitmean guard. I have trained my son to be a skilled swordsman and an excellent tactician, but the few men at arms that he has at his disposal could by no means have taken the palace by force.

"While Redge may have believed the attacks he orchestrated to be against the royal family, they were only meant to remove you and you husband's guard. The Third Order was to be disposed of in keeping with the missive I sent to the First Order. Once the Third Order and the Laitmean Guard had battered each other to pieces, and my son attained the throne, he was to sign an accord with the First Order, hidden from the public eye. Laitmea will cease to follow, capture, or punish any raiding parties once they have control of a ship. In return, the First Order will hold the lot of you silent and disseminate information regarding the abrupt change of monarch. The information contained in your old diary, as well as the queen's, would, I think, make a sufficient case if released to the public.

"Only my contact, Vee, knew the full story. She was to be responsible for both Redge's demise and the retrieval of the documents from where you quite conveniently hid them, in The Keep. I trusted no one else, *no one*, with the truth. It was, and still is, the perfect plan, and you can do nothing to stop it from running its course. "

Before anyone else could make sense of what had just been revealed, while they all stood in shock with mouths agape, Quip was moving. She spun out of her chair and launched herself at Ettalara in a blur of petticoats and anger. There was a flash of steel and a cry of pain, and as suddenly as it had begun, it was over.

Quip stepped back, panting slightly, knife in hand, daring anyone to speak. No one did. Ettalara sat as she had for the entire day, stock still, her face deathly white, while a crimson flower of blood soaked her lilac dress. Then with a small "Oh, dear," she collapsed.

* * *

Jessimin

It was clear that Ettalara was in the midst of some kind of monologue when Pippy tapped Jessimin's shoulder. She looked up to see two figures entering the hall. One was Katjia, back from stabling her horse. The other was unfamiliar, but she could only have been the pirate, Veena. She bore so little resemblance to the pretty girl at the ball that it took Jessimin several seconds to remember how she knew this. She decided at once that the loose fitting sailor's shirt didn't suit the girl at all. "Ettalara wants the Third Order destroyed," she said by way of greeting. "I don't know if she told you that she's working with the First Order to send out those records you were supposed to steal."

"The First and Third Orders will be one and the same when I retrieve them. And how do you know that?" Veena snapped, shoving Katjia into the wall and stalking towards Jessimin and Pippy.

"Door," Jessimin explained, pointing. "She talks loud."

Veena took a long, single-edged knife from her belt and pointed it at the sisters. "Since you know so much, do either of you mind telling me where those *records* are? The nomad girl was kind enough to mention that they were with someone called *Pippy*. Another of the mad Quip's progeny, no doubt."

"That would be me," said Pippy, "and you can have them." She reached into her pockets and drew out Marley's sketchbook and a hefty stack of loose-leaf paper.

Veena ripped them from her hands and shuffled through them.

"These are menus!" she screamed.

"Good menus," Pippy said, sounding affronted. "Look, there's one from when we had veal in red pepper sauce. Delicious."

"I came all the way cross-country for menus? He never even had the letters, did he? They're still in the palace somewhere, and now my chances of finding them are slim to none!"

"And there's where we had lemon tarts. I think those are what made Xeno fall in love with the baker's daughter," Pippy continued, ignoring Veena's irate screams.

"None of these explain why your dratted father is a prince. None of these are full of dirty family business! I couldn't blackmail a nun with these. How could I have fallen for such a trick? Curses upon Marley, and you, idiot nomad girl."

Katjia seemed to have recovered from being shoved and led inside at knife point, for she said, "If I'm the idiot, why are you the one screaming over last week's appetizers?"

"I'm a fool!"

"Took you long enough to work that out. But really, it's not your fault. You only have a habit of constantly underestimating people. Even if they did escape from The Tooth."

Entertaining as this show was, Jessimin couldn't help but interrupt. She had been half listening to both conversations, her ear still plastered against the doorknob.

"They've gone quiet in there," she said, flapping a hand at the other three. "I think something's wrong."

* * *

VEENA

PIPPY

The Warrior

"Oh, dear indeed!" Quip spat. "I should have made good on that promise a long time ago. But even if it be delayed by twenty years, let it be known that I kill who I say I'll kill." The madness had faded from her eyes, replaced by something more unreadable.

There should have been screaming, wailing, some kind of noise to accompany the dreadful reality in front of them, but it was silent still.

"Now to find the mysterious Vee," Quip said, though she looked on the verge of tears. "She'll hand over those diaries, or get the same... there will be no second war, whatever vile secrets we must hide to prevent it. One casualty more is one too many..."

With that, the room unfroze. Donis let out a wail and collapsed beside his dead wife. Quip absently wiped her knife blade on her skirt, Trill looking on at the scene with a mixture of disgust, relief, and sadness.

"If you want to catch Vee, you'll have to act quickly," said a small voice from the corner, and they all whirled around. A tapestry on the far wall had been pulled back to reveal a second door, and a thoroughly shocked set of twins.

"She doesn't have the diaries, and she's trying to escape into the moors," Mayzin said, her eyes glued to the corpse in its chair. "There's still enough of the Third Order out there to do some damage. She had her gentleman caller organize them around the estate. Katjia and Pippy are trying to follow them now..."

Marley was holding onto the door frame, looking distinctly green. Jessimin poked her curly head out from behind the tapestry, then just as quickly returned to hiding.

Redgenold straightened, sighing through his mustache. "I'll round them up. We don't need to worry about the low-ranking pirates right now. Who's their leader, and what does he look like?"

"His name is Carsten," Marley said, "chestnut hair, tan skin, quite tall. Rides a gray horse with a white spot on its rump."

"Good enough. I'll catch the little blighter before he makes it a mile. I'm taking one of your horses, Donis. You won't miss it where you're going, anyway."

Redge stormed out of the room, leaving stony silence in his wake.

Trilliapa was the first to speak, walking over to the twins and Jessimin. "I think we'll spend the night here, and head back home in the morning. You three probably already have rooms set up here; let me walk you upstairs and get you settled."

She took Jessimin and Marley by their hands, leading them down the hall towards the stairs. "There's some books in my luggage if you want to read while we sort things out here. I'm sure you don't want to stick around for arrests and accusations."

She padded up the plush carpeted steps, her skirts swishing in a comforting sort of way. "I've seen my fair share of violent horrors, but it still makes my stomach turn and my heart try to beat its way out of my chest. It's alright if none of you want to talk about it, but if you do, come find me. Just because I'm queen doesn't mean I can't be your aunty too."

Mayzin picked up Marley's book from where it had fallen in the hall, then hurried after Trill. They came to the rooms in which they had been staying, and there the queen let them go.

"It won't mean anything to you now, but you should know, your mother never wanted any of her children to see something like that. Neither of us wanted that.

"We like to pretend that we left those horrible things in a past life, but sometimes, there's nothing we can do about it. The bloodshed finds us, one way or another. I'm going to find Evayah and Donis III now, if any of you need me." With that, she departed, leaving them to the peace of the second floor hall.

For a time, all three of them stood looking over the balcony. They watched Katjia and Pippy return, only to be ushered upstairs by the king. They watched Redgenold return with Carsten and Veena trussed like chickens on the back of his horse. They saw the butler arrested too, and the other servants presenting themselves for interrogation. They saw men arriving from the city of Firdell and, at last, removing a shrouded form from the sitting room.

"When Veena grabbed those menus, I laughed," Jessimin said, after a while. "I didn't know that Aunt Ettalara was being stabbed. While she was dying, I was laughing."

Mayzin wrapped an arm around her, resting her chin on Jessimin's shoulder. "I watched it happen. I knew what mother was about to do, and I didn't turn away. I just kept on holding that tapestry open a chink to see."

"I closed my eyes," Marley whispered. "I knew she was a traitor meeting a fitting end, but I couldn't bring myself to see it happen. I closed my eyes as tightly as I could, and kept them closed."

"I suppose we've all learned a lesson in not romanticizing mother and Aunty Trill's pasts. What terrible things they must have seen to look at that and not be sick," Jessimin sighed, "I shouldn't have run to see what was happening."

"I hope Evayah is alright," said Mayzin, "and I'm glad she wasn't watching."

"She'll survive," said Marley, "We all will. Veena's plot was foiled, and there won't be any more bloodshed. No second war, no more death. We'll all be just fine." He looked at the bloodstained armchair being pushed out of the parlor, and added, "Eventually."

* * *

Mayzin

Mother has killed Aunty Ettalara. I don't know how to feel about it all. She was the mastermind behind the plot that lead to Marley's kidnapping, Addmaleta's near assassination, and Redge's bid for kingship. She was Veena's informant, and wanted to put her own son on the throne.

I know that if she had been justly tried, the outcome would have been the same. That level of treason can only lead to the noose. But she was still my Aunty for all of my life. It's strange to think that the woman who was so kind and so calm with all us little princes and princesses was holding so much hate in her heart.

Mother says that it was all laid out in her diary. Not the letters between her and Veena, of course. Those came much later. But her diary from when she was fifteen, traipsing across all Eretz with Mother and Aunty Trill. After all of the scheming to get evidence against them, she forgot about the evidence against herself. She showed who she really was in those pages. Somebody who was afraid of suffering, willing to sell out her friends at a moment's notice, woefully unaware of the pain she caused others, happy to lie, cheat, and deceive. She always put on a pretty face for company, but what little introspection she did was shallow at best.

Of course, those are Mother's thoughts. If someone were to make a list of *her* faults, I'm sure it wouldn't make for pleasant reading either. Stubborn, tight-lipped, and too self assured, for one. Maybe a little insane, or maybe she just doesn't care enough about the opinions of others to ever bother reining herself in. She could do with a little more thought before speaking, too.

Uncle Dowlin will face the same fate as his wife, soon. Ettalara said that he wasn't privy to her plans, but there's a boldfaced lie if ever I saw one. He lived in her house, he ate at her table, and he had access to all of her letters, even the ones from Veena. If he was ignorant, it was willfully so. Their children won't be punished, for Evayah is not yet of age, and Donis III was manipulated against his will, much the same as Redgie. The lot of them will be stripped of their titles, but they can live out their days in peace as long as they don't cause any more trouble.

Veena and Carsten are subject to pirate law, not ours, but their king, Zavaxer (horrible moniker, if you ask me) sent word that we can execute them ourselves. There's too many things that could go wrong if we tried to send them back to Mer. One midnight ambush on the road is enough for years to come. The rest of the Third Order have vanished into the hills and we've let them go. They can all marry peasants and start a new life here. If they return to Mer, they will be put to death for treason against Zavaxer, and I'm sure they all know it.

Nobody else has or will be harmed. I suppose it's the best ending anyone could have hoped for, but really, I can't help but think that it's just one more chapter in the story Darin the Terrible started when he killed his family and stole the throne. I wish that I could say that we'll be free of war now, but even if fate didn't take such an interest in our family, I know that there will be more death and destruction to come.

Maudlin thoughts, I know, but then, Ettalara's bloody end has put me in that mood. I think I'll go talk to Marley. It's better than sitting in my room here ruminating on death, anyway.

* * *

Kanara

Kanara watched through the window as the king and queen came up the palace drive. Katjia was with them, safe and sound once more. He had been angry beyond words when she had left so soon again after he had discovered that she was still alive. Now, he understood and was proud of what she had accomplished.

She had been strong and smart enough to evade the pirates, foil their plots, and keep the prince safe. She was his little sister.

He turned away, and came face to face with Princess Addmaleta. She gave him a shy smile and tucked a lock of her hair behind one ear. Kanara still could not believe that he had become so close to the first heir to the Laitmean throne.

Despite her mother's warnings, Addmaleta had sought him out after the assassination attempt and struck up a conversation. Her company had helped to pass the long hours trapped in the palace, while their sibling and cousin led pirates halfway across the country. She was pretty, funny, and completely open. Every time he looked at her, he could not help but marvel.

He knew that she felt much the same. Baffling as it was, she found his company as enjoyable as he found hers. The only dark spot in this otherwise perfect picture was the news that they had received: Onkay's days of famine were numbered. The rains were beginning to fall again, and soon grass would be springing up around the once-dry pools. In another time, this would have made Kanara the happiest man alive. Now, it hurt him to his core.

"Have you decided if you're returning to Onkay?"

"I'm my family's leader, even if I'm not very good at it. I don't know that I have much of a choice. I just wish it wouldn't mean never seeing you again."

"Never is a very strong word," the princess remarked, walking to the widow to watch the carriages parking.

"I would never see you again in this capacity," he amended.

"What capacity is that?"

Kanara felt himself growing hot, and he tugged at his collar, still unbalanced by Addmaleta's forward nature. "If I return, it will be as someone else. I would take a wife from among my people, and you a husband. This sort of conversation between us would no longer be appropriate. Our friendship will be a distant one if I return to Onkay, and not just because of the intervening miles."

Addmaleta was frowning, and he had the sense that she no longer saw what was before her.

"I don't want that," she said at last. "I would prefer something much closer. More than close—more than friendship."

Kanara studied her profile, illuminated by the window.

"I don't want it either," he said.

"But it can't be," Addmaleta said, "you're honor bound to see your family safely home, aren't you?"

Kanara looked away, to where Katjia was tending to the coach horses, while Marley carried her things inside.

"Not necessarily," he said, past a lump in his throat. "Perhaps, someone else could take my place, and do it better than me."

Addmaleta whirled around to face him. "Then don't go. Marry me."

He stared at her for what felt like an eternity, then caught her in his arms, and whispered, "Yes, princess."

* * *

Marley

We're back home once again. Funnily enough, it doesn't really feel like home any more. Maybe it has something to do with the two dragons on the roof or the number of servants who are gone or Ettalara's death. I'm not even writing an explanation of what's transpired. Mayzin can do that for both of us.

Maybe it has more to do with the fact that I never felt particularly at home here to begin with. The only thing that ever made life here tolerable was Mayzin. I still feel at home when I'm with her, but that's not a good reason to make this particular palace my abode.

I've felt far more *at home* these past few weeks, despite being kidnapped by pirates, escaping on dragonback, and being thrown into every manner of unfamiliar circumstances. Even now, I feel most at home in the nomad's camp in the courtyard. I could spend days listening to Katjia's small cousins chatter. I could spend a lifetime eating the simple food they cook, and listening to the old stories that they tell. They wear simpler clothes, speak simpler words, and never look at me as if I have two heads when I voice an opinion on something.

None of them have hidden motivations for what they say. None of them expect me to remember why they're feuding with their second cousin twice removed. None of them expect me to know whose great-grandchildren they are, and they certainly don't care if I know what cut of dress was popular last season and why it isn't popular now.

Everyone knows that Katjia and I are courting, in a manner of speaking. Her brother is pleased with us, as far as I can tell. Unlike some Laitmeans, they don't have any taboo against outsiders in the tribe. Kanara spends most of his time with cousin Addmaleta, anyway. I suspect that they are waiting for the perfect moment to announce their engagement.

I've been talking with Mayzin, and she says that as soon as I come of age, I should join the nomads in the desert. I was quite surprised. I thought that she would want to keep me in the capital forever; she is my twin, after all. But she said that she's never seen me so happy. I'd need to find a way of keeping my skin from burning to a crisp, but on the whole I like the idea.

I'm not so sure I want to leave Mayzin entirely. We have our differences, but we've always gotten along well, and in truth, she was my only friend for many years. She said that she would be happy enough as long as I visited once a year. She said that I could do it easily enough with Eldrid. I think she might be right, seeing as the dragon has become extraordinarily placid. She spends most of her time with Dart, but she can be coaxed to do almost anything if provided sufficient cheese. On dragonback, I could cover the distance from Onkay to Lyrah in just a day.

I'll continue to think on the matter. I know mother and father would give their blessing on the proposition now, if I asked. I do feel sorry for them that Xeno is their most ordinary son. One thrown out for treason, one thinking of throwing away his title to become a nomad, and one whose worst crime is eating a few too many pastries. I fear that it is a good thing that Xeno is not directly in line for the crown, for he shows every sign of becoming a snobby noble.

At least the girls are normal. Even Kestly has amended her lawless ways a bit. I think she was afraid that she'd be stripped of her title like Redge, for she has recently 'found' several pieces of Addmaleta's jewelry that were missing. She still slips out of windows more than is strictly good for her, but then again, so does Queen Trilliapa, and nobody ever says anything about that. It's best not to argue with someone who has a pet dragon.

* * *

Veena

There is no reason for me to finish this account, except to pass the time. No one will read it. Perhaps my uncle was only playing to my pride when he said that this would make the grandest addition to pirate lore, but for a time, I believed it.

What more is there to say? Marley and Katjia never had the documents. I fell for their bait like a fool. Had I gone ahead as planned, Carsten would be King of the Pirates and Donis Atticus Cornelius III would be King of Laitmea. With Princess Ettalara Annalee of Firdell as my informant, how could I have failed? Everything I knew of Laitmean politics and power came from her. It was a foolproof plan. But what I didn't bargain on was insanity. Who could place bets on the capricious nature of the mad Quip?

Ettalara is dead. Quip stabbed her through the heart in her home. There wasn't a soul alive who deserved it more. She betrayed her closest friends, her family, and her country. There never was such a complete and utter betrayal before, especially not after everything the three women went through together; Quip, Trill, and Lara, the girls who rewrote the course of history. A thing like that would have driven me mad, too.

I heard the scene play out through a keyhole, and even now, I see it in my mind's eye. They all knew, the king, the queen, their guard and lady. They had planned to bring her in quietly and execute her after full trial. But Quip never could keep a handle on her own convictions, and loyalty was the strongest one of them all. For Ettalara to break her trust and deceive her must have cut her deeper than any physical wound, for such things go against the very fiber of her being. They say she is a madwoman, but perhaps she is the sanest one of us all. She saw a thing that she could not abide, and she dealt with it to the best of her abilities.

I don't resent Quip's actions. I admire Marley's. It is a rare soul who can best me at my own game.

This may be the first and last entry in which I am completely honest. For goodness sake, I started writing things down to keep track of my lies. But now, I feel the need to see a record of the truth, if only so I do not come off as completely incompetent.

Redgenold was caught by the palace guard in the hills just west of the capital. His sister Kestly tracked him down, on orders from three more of his sisters, who had worked out a small part of what he intended from letters that he failed to burn. Am I a fool, that parts of my scheme were uncovered by children? They are Quip's children. I had the misfortune to pick an enemy who had four small copies of herself to be her eyes and ears in the palace.

The Third Order has scattered to the four winds. Carsten's men are traitors by both Laitmean and pirate law. If they are caught, the consequences will be severe. I doubt that they will be, though. Most are smart enough to avoid notice. They will find quiet, simple lives among the peasants, if they have any sense.

A few are foolish enough to brag about the warriors that they once were. Only suffering waits for them, but it's not as if their lot would have been much different staying with us. Donis's army would have needed some bodies to show that they had effectively routed Redgenold's planned coup.

Carsten is a different story. Did I ever really love him? Or was he just a convenient way to get back at my Uncle? Even now, I don't know the answers to these questions. I know that he loved me and will go to his grave with my name on his lips. I suppose I should feel guilty for leading him into all of this; they're going to execute him tomorrow. He is too violent, too dangerous, too difficult to imprison. He was a wanted man in every country I know of for some reason or another. Treason, piracy, murder, he's done them all.

Laitmea is renewing their bonds of friendship with King Zavaxer. Disposing of Carsten will go a long way towards winning his undying respect. He will change how the pirates live, there is no doubt about it. I would hate to see a world in which we leave ships to keep their own course and eke our living out of the shoreline. Fishing is not business enough for me, and this *legitimate enterprise* will not bring Mer the wealth she deserves. Zavaxer will say that it is all for the best, and that Pirate's Cove should only be a name on a map. Maybe it will bring more prosperity in the long run to have cordial relations with our neighbors. But if that is the state of things, it is probably best that I am leaving.

Of course, I am not going the way I would have liked to. Shot down in battle, poisoned by my enemies, but not tried and executed in an honest court of law. It's not becoming for a pirate. The trial part is over, anyway. Every soul in Laitmea knows that I am guilty of a plot against my own government and theirs, and quite frankly, Onkay's too. I employed methods that were… *dishonest, unnecessarily cruel, vile, and like to war crimes.* Ettalara hadn't burned my letters either, so there were heaps of evidence against me. No, it's no surprise at all. A sad end, but no surprise.

I'll accept my fate with as much equanimity as I have, which is more than most. I achieved all I really needed to, anyway, when my Uncle breathed his last. Someone else can finish this sorry story later, if they ever find the first half of it.

And that is the honest end to the account of Veena the Pirate.

* * *

Katjia

Katjia stood by the gate, trying to understand what it was that she was feeling.

"Katte?" Kanara set a hand on her shoulder. "There have been travelers and traders down in the city. They say that the month after we left, the rains returned. Not much, but enough to make the desert sing."

Katjia turned to face her brother, realizing that her heart was full of apprehension. "You don't want to return, do you?"

"No. Katte, you must understand. However hard I try, I am not the leader that our family deserves. You can tell me that it is all in my head, but even if you are right, does that make me the sort of man you want in charge?"

"You haven't called me Katte since I was a little girl."

"Do you not like it?"

"It only reminds me how much older I am. I want to go back to the desert, but I cannot make the trek on my own."

"I don't intend for you to do so. You should take the whole family and Prince Marley, if he wants to go."

"Me?"

"You will be a good leader. One who can make important decisions without doubt. Without fear of whether you are wrong. Katte, you have never once doubted yourself. I know I've called you rash for it, but it is your best quality."

"If I lead them back to the desert and leave you here, will I ever see you again? I cannot leave my big brother, even if he is the future King of Laitmea."

"Will you stop making cheese?"

"Will the sun halt in the sky? Our people have made cheese for a thousand thousands of years."

"Then you will see me quite frequently," he said, gesturing at the palace roof. Around the highest tower, a massive purple dragon was curled.

Katjia smiled, and hugged Kanara as tightly as she could. "Then we will leave after the wedding."

"Good."

* * *

Mayzin

After everything that's happened, I think that no one in my family ought to write a diary for a very long time. It just invites terrible events and strange people into our lives.

Marley will probably keep writing until he dies, seeing as the past few weeks have brought him adventures on ships, dragon riding, and the love of his life. Personally, I think I'll stop after today. It's been an interesting exercise, but I hate the thought of all my personal business being kept in a book that anyone could pick up and read. More to the point, even if it's helped me sort through my thoughts, the risks seem to outweigh the benefits.

Marley says that I'm being superstitious, and that keeping a diary doesn't automatically guarantee that you'll have strange happenings to fill it with, but I'd like to think that anyone who reads this would agree that it's just not worth taking the chance. I'll buy a lock for this book and put it in the tower with all of our other incriminating evidence. It can gather dust until one of my descendants has the fool thought of keeping a diary.

Frankly, I'm only writing now because I know Pippy reads what I write, and she'll be hopping mad if I leave her without a conclusion.

I wrote Bella a very long letter the other day, apologizing for not responding to her last letter. She wrote back in characteristic Bella fashion. I'll put it in here along with her other letters, so there won't just be one family's dirty laundry hiding in the dragon tower.

218

A hoard of gold is fine, but what Dart really loves guarding is gossip, and it seems that Eldrid is much the same. Jessi can tell them all her secrets, and if it comes to it, so can I. And that, dear reader, is the end of my foray into introspective writing. I'm off to buy a lock and some cheese.

* * *

Dearest Mayzin,

I'd be out of sorts too, if I had a brother go missing, and an Aunty murdered. I hear that they've had everyone involved with the plots executed, except your fool brother. Maybe it's deserved, but my, that's not a pleasant end. Once again, I'm glad that I'm away from it all, and I can't blame Marley for wanting to leave either.

I know it all falls on deaf ears, of course. You wouldn't leave the aristocracy for anything in the world. But even you can admit that it's not a pretty thing when a prince and a pirate are hung for their crimes. I'm glad they let Redgie off. He's mad as a hatter, and probably dangerous, but I don't think it's right to kill a person who didn't understand their own deeds. He was manipulated, by Vee and everyone else.

I'd like to leave you with happy news (you know me), but I'm sure you've already gathered that Finny and I are expecting a child. A happy little peasant, who'll never have to worry about their Uncle's wife plotting to have them killed. Granted, neither Finny nor I have brothers, or anyone close enough to call a brother, but all the same, I'm happy that my child won't grow up knowing about all the gossip and the plots.

I'd love to have you out to visit, sometime. I know our current accommodations aren't as grand as anything you're used to, but everything is clean and bright and the pantry is well-stocked. You can meet the baby and all the goats we're keeping. It's not all that far for you to come, especially if there's a spare dragon you can ride. Give your family my condolences and love,

Bella

* * *

Dear Bella,

I'm so very happy for you. I'll definitely accept your offer to host me. I'm amenable to small and clean houses and meeting your baby. I'm less sure about the goats.

Before everything happened, I'm sure your words would have fallen on deaf ears, but after so many terrible plots and executions, I'm beginning to think that my jewels and fine dresses aren't worth all that. Perhaps there's some happy middle ground—rich, but outside of the politics and the danger.

Anyway, Father has been hiring new servants to replace the lot from Aunty Ettalara. They seem much the same, except for the new under-butler. He's Haputian, with red hair, green eyes, and a lovely voice. I'll leave you to draw your own conclusions.

Warm Regards,

Lady Mayzin

* * *

Marley

Kanara is going to marry Addmaleta, to no one's surprise. It means that he will someday be King Consort, a lofty title for someone who spent his whole life tending horses in the desert. I started out with a lofty title, though, and I will soon be leaving to tend horses in the desert.

No, I'm not of age, but after everything that's happened, nobody cares. If anyone asks, my family will just say that I need time to recover from my imprisonment. Frankly, I found imprisonment better than the parties I had to attend as Prince Marley.

Katjia is going to lead her family, now that her brother is indisposed— married. She's not of age by our law, but that doesn't matter in Onkay. Tribe leaders are voted upon by the families. Usually, they're the oldest sons of the last leader, but it's not required. She'll do well. Luckily, if *we* are married, I will not have to become Tribe-leader-consort. I would be hopeless at it.

We leave directly after the wedding. I have inherited Kanara's horse, which funnily enough is Petrushka's brother, Petrarch.

If Mayzin ever wants to see me, though, my steed will be Eldrid. All Mayzin needs to do is tell her to find me, and Eldrid will go looking for the man who introduced her to cheese.

I think that I will leave my diary behind. There won't be much time for writing, anyway. Food needs to be made, horses must be tended to, and Katjia will want to talk. It doesn't matter much what we say, as long as we're talking together. I suppose everyone should find someone they can talk to that way. It makes for a good life.

Writing was a fun experiment, anyway. Mayzin thinks it's what made the pirates attack and Aunty Ettalara die, but I know better. Nobody ever needs help to cause mayhem and destruction. It's only human nature. This diary is just one more record of it, the same as every other book that's ever been written. Except Aunty Ettalara's old book of etiquette. That's a record of something more terrible all together, best left to the foul pits from whence it came.

I'll soon be closer to the southern coast than the northern one, which will be interesting. Katjia has promised to show me the ships that sail there. I'd have had a harder time agreeing to go to the desert if her family's seasonal treks didn't pass by a few ports. As it is, I'll not be riding on any ships (a relief after the legendary seasickness of Pirate's Cove), but I'll be seeing my fill of southern freighters. They're all together different from the river ships and the pirate vessels of the north, so perhaps I'll need a new sketchbook.

Come to think of it, that's what this diary was supposed to be. There's still plenty of pages left, so I'll just be tearing these first few out and giving them to Mayzin. She can have a laugh once I'm gone. Not much of a conclusion, but then, conclusions never stopped more things from happening. This is just—goodbye for now.

Marley Michaell Fredrick.

* * *

Jessimin

Jessimin was once again dozing off at a party. She decided to take inventory of her siblings again, just to be sure that they were all present and accounted for. Redge, of course, was not in attendance. He had been sentenced to five years of labor in a mine, on top of losing his title. Jessimin suspected that the work would improve him greatly.

Lara was sitting with her husband, probably debating whether she should stop using her middle name from now on. Kestly was sitting on a windowsill, looking like she desperately wanted to climb out until a handsome young man came to ask her to dance. If she wasn't much mistaken, Jessimin suspected that his name was Tobias.

Xeno was once again making short work of the pastry bar, to no one's surprise, and Pippy was dancing with Duke Javis's son.

Marley was happily telling Katjia about a type of ship that he hoped to see off the southern coast of Onkay, and Mayzin was doing nothing at all. Except perhaps keeping a closer eye than was strictly necessary on the new under-butler. But maybe that was just her imagination running away with her.

Aunty Trill was sitting on her throne at the head of the room, deep in conversation with her mother. Though a pang shot through her at the sight of an Aunty Ettalara-free meeting, Jessimin had to admit that Marley had been right. They were all going to be just fine.

Not today, probably not tomorrow, but someday soon, the memories of Ettalara's demise would not seem so sharp and painful. They would always carry something of that day with them, but they would all be just fine.

Then she shifted her gaze to the party's guests of honor. No diplomat, no stunningly beautiful niece, just her cousin Addmaleta and Katjia's brother Kanara, celebrating their wedding. The day was bittersweet, for it marked the end of the nomads' stay in the courtyard. They would be leaving for the desert tomorrow, and taking Marley with them.

Jessimin was sure that there wasn't a better ending possible. Everyone was happy, the traitors and treasonous plotters were dead, romance was in the air.

Yet somehow, she was still bored. Rising from the table, Jessimin made her way to the back of the room, where the king and queen resided. Maybe she should have learned better than to listen in on her family's conversations, but mother and Trill were *so* intent on whatever it was that they were talking about, and the party was *so* boring…

* * *

The Thief

Queen Trilliapa was reclining on her throne, sipping a glass of red wine and nibbling on a slice of pear. She had actually ordered several fragrant cheeses to be served with the wine, but an hour before the wedding banquet, her chef had informed her that there was no cheese left in the palace.

"If lack of cheese is the worst calamity of the day, I'd say the new couple's life is off to a very promising start," Quipeneay whispered in her ear, cutting a chunk off her own pear with her knife.

Trill nodded absently. "I still remember my own wedding like it was yesterday. Now it's Addmaleta out on the dance floor. Gets you thinking, doesn't it?"

"If you say so," Quip mumbled through a too big bite of pear.

After a moment, the queen reached up and rapped the blade of her knife with a knuckle.

"This knife was made for Darin, before he was king. It was the weapon he intended to use to kill his sister Hillena, but she escaped and carried on the royal line in her daughter, Ettalara.

"When you stabbed her, it was as if it had finally reached its target, done what it was made to do. It was meant to be, I think. I don't know if that knife would ever have been sated until it ended Hillena's bloodline."

"That's a lot of emotion to attach to a piece of metal that's been up my sleeve since I was seven," Quip said, leaning on the back of Trill's throne. "I didn't want to kill her, but that's no reason to say that the blade did the deed. I was the one wielding it."

"You never did believe in curses or superstitions, did you?" Trill asked.

"Why should I? There's not one compelling piece of evidence to say that fate or destiny exist. No one pulls our strings but us. Do you think otherwise?"

"Do I think otherwise? Just listen to us, using big words like destiny and otherwise. How could I think differently? We both came from nothing, didn't we? No fate worth its salt would choose us to be the instruments of fortune, yet here we are. All grown up and philosophical."

"Now there's a word that's just too big," Quip snorted, "it's a shame my knife can't cut *philosophical* down to size. How do you know that it was Darin's, anyway?"

"Those letters. The ones Veena was after."

"Redge's Uncle Efin sent us those years ago. They were from his mother, before she died and left him in the orphanage. What have they got to say about Darin?"

"You never read them very carefully, did you?" Trill asked.

"No, I never felt the need. You said they were good enough to make me a princess, and I left it at that."

"Well, put them together with our old diaries, and you get quite a story. It's no wonder Veena thought she could oust us by making them public knowledge."

"And what do you propose to do with them, my queen?"

Trill tapped on the arm of her throne, thoughtful.

"I've been considering a bit of a project, honestly. Addmaleta will be taking up a good number of royal affairs, now that she's of age and wed. I'll have the time to do some digging, on Darin and others. Seeing death again, after so many years of peace, really set me to thinking: Where does it all come from? War, death, all the horrors like that."

"Sounds like a cheery topic," Quip laughed, "but if it brings you peace of mind, by all means, study away. It's only a shame you don't have Ettalara's old diaries to add to the mix. I have a feeling they would have made for interesting reading."

"Oh, I have those, too. It's probably half the reason she wanted to break into The Keep, too. Didn't like that I had so much of her dirty laundry."

"But how? If I remember correctly, she threw her first diary into a moat while I was in the hospital recovering from plague fever."

"That, Quip, is the benefit of having a pet dragon. Dart fished that book out in under a minute. It was drying off in his toasty warm tummy before the guards even caught up with us."

Quip tilted her knife, and watched the candlelight glint off of it. "We really haven't changed at all, have we? We're still just a pair of terrified teenagers, trying to make our way in the world."

"War will do that to a person. Although I have to say, I've gotten better at lacing my corset. It doesn't hurt anymore."

"Me too. And my knife-throwing skills, vastly improved."

"I'm a better pickpocket than I ever was in Haputa, though only because I've had to return so many things without letting on that I stole them in the first place."

"I even remember what spoon to use when I'm eating."

"Now that, I'm still working on."

* * *

THE PALACE

Epilogue

A little girl climbed onto the palace roof. Her skin was the color of fine imported coffee, her eyes bright blue as the sky, and her hair a mass of pencil thin amber-gold ringlets. She was wearing a very fine dress, marred only by the dirt stains around her knees.

She dusted herself off, and called out in a singsong voice, "I have cheese!"

The reaction was instantaneous. Three small dragons skittered across the tiles, one purple and two green, all with orange eyes. The girl laughed as they circled around her, flapping their wings and squeaking with excitement. She tossed pieces of cheese from her pockets, and the trio descended upon them, tails wagging. She patted them clumsily on their heads, saying "good dragons, good dragons."

"What are you doing up here, Lissabet?"

A young woman was sitting between the crenelations on the edge of the roof, watching.

"Feeding the dragons, Aunty Jessimin."

"Eldrid gives them plenty, dearest."

"I know, but I like to talk to them."

"So do I."

"What do you tell them about?" the little girl asked, curious.

"Oh, this and that. How my day is going, what people in the palace are saying. I tell Eldrid about the letters I get from Uncle Marley. She's very fond of him."

"Why?"

229

"Has no one told you that story?" Jessimin patted a spot on the wall beside her. "Come, sit." The little girl trotted over.

"Your Uncle Marley," she said, "was the first person to give Eldrid cheese. It happened years ago, on a little island far to the north…"

The three little dragons scampered over to hear the story. They couldn't understand Jessimin's words, but somewhere in their orange eyes, one could see a certain spark. They weren't going to believe a tall tale in which dragons hadn't always eaten cheese.

* * *

Pronunciation Guide

Eretz (AIR-ets): The continent on which our story takes place.
  Haputa (huh-poo-tuh): The smallest country in the land of Eretz.
  Styllyg (STIL-igg): The land of the long grass.

Mer (MER): The land of the pirates.
  Veena (VEE-nuh): A pirate.
  Carsten (car-stun): Veena's gentleman caller.
  Zavaxer (ZAH-vah-zeer): The king of the pirates.
  Serafina (Sir-AH-fin-uh): Veena's mother.

Onkay (On-KAY): The desert land.
  Katjia (KAHT-sha): A nomad girl.
  Kanara (can-ARE-uh): Katjia's brother.
  Petrushka (puh-TRU-shka): Katjia's horse.
  Petrarch (PET-rar-sh): Kanara's horse.

Laitmea (LAY-it-MAY-ah): The largest country in the land of Eretz.
  Lyrah (LIE-rah): The capital of Laitmea.
  Dowlin (DOW-lin): The King of Laitmea.
  Trilliapa (TRILL-ee-YUH-pa): The Queen of Laitmea.
  Addmaleta (ADD-ma-LEE-ta): The crown princess of Laitmea.
  Alloysius (AL-oh-WHISH-us): Addmaleta's youngest brother.
  Quipeneay (QUIP-in-YAY): Queen Trilliapa's personal bodyguard and

princess.

Redgenold (REG-un-OLD): Prince and Captain of Laitmea's guard.

Jessimin (JES-ih-MIN): Quipeneay and Redgenold's youngest daughter.

Mayzin (MAY-zyn): Quipeneay and Redgenold's second youngest daughter.

Marley (MAR-lee): Mayzin's twin brother.

Kestly (kess-LEE):Quipeneay and Redgenold's second oldest daughter.

Xeno (ZEE-no):Quipeneay and Redgenold's second oldest son.

Efin (ef-IN): Redgenold's uncle.

Donis (DAW-niss): The King's brother.

Ettalara (ETA-la-RA): Donis's wife.

Evayah (UH-vay-uh): Donis and Ettalara's daughter.

Elisabet (E-lis-U-bett): The late queen of Laitmea, Donis and Dowlin's' mother.

Acknowledgment

Anybody who's read my acknowledgments before will know that they are sheer chaos. I don't subscribe to the theory that this section of a book needs to be boring and formulaic. The reader surely doesn't gain any appreciation for these people if they're forced to slog through a mundane list of names. It needs spice! It needs pizzazz!

The world needs to know that I wrote these right after trying to explain the plot to my mom, who loves me, but not fantasy. Thanks to her! And Dad! And everybody else who patiently bore my obsession with this project!

Next, thanks to everyone who supported the Kickstarter project. Here are your names, as promised, in no particular order:

Andrea, James, Ingrid, Kevin, Tante Tina, Sister in Christ!

And of course, Oma, Opa, and Grandma. Your monetary contributions are greatly appreciated. Have a bonus smiley face :)

Thanks to my underpaid proofreader, Anna, without whom this book would be rather typo heavy.

Thanks to the dog, for being fuzzy.

Really, at this point in the proceedings, only about ten percent of you are still reading* I could start thanking anyone! Bwahahahaha!

'til next time,

BelaJane

*(this is a totally made up statistic with zero research to back it up.)

P.S.

If you're still reading this, Thank *you*.

About the Author

BelaJane Crilly is the author of several halfway decent fantasy novels. She lives outside of Chicago and currently attends college for several subjects only tangentially related to creative writing. Her loved ones frequently accuse her of 'selling herself short,' but this is her bio and she can say whatever she likes.

You can connect with me on:

- https://belajanebooks.weebly.com
- https://twitter.com/belajanecrilly
- https://instagram.com/belajanecrilly

Also by BelaJane Crilly

The Lady, The Thief, and The Warrior

Amid a landscape of bloodshed and skirmishes, Ettalara, a young noblewoman, sets out to return crucial documents to her king. Despite a path fraught with danger, dragons, and dances, she forges ahead. But when she meets Quip and Trill, a pair of orphans with a decidedly different view of the war, her plans may come crashing to a halt.

Coming Soon! The Dagger, The Book, and The Crown.

Desperate to understand the horrors she has faced, Queen Trilliapa sets out to uncover the truth about what first drove her nation to war. From the southern cliffs to the archipelago of doom, the marks of battle are fading fast, yet the letters, diary entries, and fragments of poetry left behind hint at deeper story. There are answers for her to find, but not all are as she expects…

www.ingramcontent.com/pod-product-compliance
Lightning Source LLC
Chambersburg PA
CBHW060632260626
47161CB00008B/2867